The First Time Ever Published!

The Eleventh Donut Shop Mystery

From *New York Times* Bestselling Author

Jessica Beck

ASSAULT AND BATTER

Books by Jessica Beck

The Donut Shop Mysteries

Glazed Murder
Fatally Frosted
Sinister Sprinkles
Evil Éclairs
Tragic Toppings
Killer Crullers
Drop Dead Chocolate
Powdered Peril
Illegally Iced
Deadly Donuts
ASSAULT AND BATTER

The Classic Diner Mysteries

A Chili Death
A Deadly Beef
A Killer Cake
A Baked Ham
A Bad Egg
A Real Pickle

The Ghost Cat Cozy Mysteries

Ghost Cat: Midnight Paws
Ghost Cat 2: Bid for Midnight

Jessica Beck is the *New York Times* Bestselling Author
of
The Donut Shop Mysteries
as well as
The Classic Diner Mysteries
and
The Ghost Cat Cozy Mysteries

ASSAULT AND BATTER by Jessica Beck:
Copyright © 2013

All rights reserved.

To P and E,
Always!

Chapter 1

Like a great many things in life, it started with a wedding.

Or is that where it all ended?

All I really know is that when the dead body appeared, it looked as though *everything* would be ruined.

It's all very hard to explain, but one thing is certain: I knew that after what happened that day, my life, and the lives of many of the folks around me in April Springs, North Carolina, would never be the same.

But as usual, I'm getting ahead of myself.

Let me back up a bit and start at the beginning.

Chapter 2

"Suzanne, do you have a second?" Emily Hargraves had walked into Donut Hearts a few minutes earlier, but she hadn't been able to make eye contact with me since she came through the door. Emily owned our local newsstand, Two Cows and a Moose, and I'd been friends with the pretty young brunette for years—even babysitting her once upon a time—as hard as that was for me to believe. She was lovely, especially when she smiled, but her grin was absent at the moment.

"Is anything wrong?" I asked her softly as I refilled Ray Blake's coffee cup. Ray was the father of my lone employee, Emma, and the editor of our local newspaper.

"You're going to have to be the one to tell me that. I've been putting something off for days, but it can't wait any longer." That sounded serious. If whatever Emily had to say was confidential, I doubted that it was good idea to say it in front of Ray.

"Give me one second," I said as I held up one finger. Opening the door into the kitchen, I found Emma elbows deep in dirty dishes, her iPod earbuds nestled firmly in her ears. Shouting probably wouldn't have been enough to get her attention, so I tapped her on the shoulder.

"Suzanne, you scared the daylights out of me," Emma said as she pulled one earbud out. "What's going on?"

"I need you to cover the front, but there's something even more important that you need to do for me if you can."

"Anything. Just name it," she said with a smile. Emma had quit the donut shop for a little while, but now she was back where she belonged. I knew her tenure with me wouldn't last forever, but as long as it did, I was going to enjoy it.

"I need you to keep your dad from leaving the shop for the next few minutes. Can you do that?"

"Dad's up front?" she asked. "Why didn't he come back and say hello?"

"You'll have to ask him that," I said. "Can you do it?"

"Oh, yes," she said with the hint of a wicked grin.

"Should I even ask you how you're going to do it?" I asked her.

"Well, there's no reason that I can't have a little fun with him, is there?" Emma asked me.

"No reason at all," I replied, returning her smile with one of my own. I had a love/hate relationship with Ray Blake most of the time. His obsession with breaking news had caused a few rifts between Emma and me over the years, and I always knew who was responsible for them. Still, I understood that he loved his daughter completely, and ultimately I couldn't hold his fierceness against him.

I followed Emma out of the kitchen, and after she said hello to Emily, my employee said, "Dad, we need to talk."

He nearly choked on his coffee as he started to stand. "What's going on, Emma?"

"You'd better sit back down," she said gravely.

I was torn between talking to Emily and hearing what Emma was about to say, but the newsstand owner touched my arm lightly. "Suzanne, can we go outside?"

"That would be perfect," I said.

Ray didn't even notice as Emily and I slipped outside. I figured that Emma would buy us a few minutes of privacy, and I really couldn't afford to waste a moment of it.

"Let's sit out here," I said as I motioned to one of my outside tables. It was late autumn and the leaves were mostly gone, but the air still had a crisp freshness that I adored. Soon enough the weather would turn too cold for lingering time spent outside, but for now, it was just about perfect.

I took a seat at the table, and Emily sat across from

me.

"Okay, you've got my attention. Now, tell me what's wrong."

"Nothing, actually. Well, that's not entirely true. There's one thing that's casting a bit of gloom on everything."

"Tell me what it is, and I'll do my best to fix it," I said with my brightest smile. I was a big fan of Emily and her three stuffed animals that spawned the name of her shop, Two Cows and a Moose, and I'd do anything I could to make her happy.

"Honestly, it's you," she said, her voice nearly cracking.

I frowned in puzzlement. "Me? How am I causing you pain?"

"It's not *actually* you," she said. "It's so hard to find the right words to say. I knew that this was all going to come out wrong."

"Emily, take a deep breath, and then just tell me whatever is on your mind. We've been friends for too long for anything to come between us."

"But don't you see? That's what makes this so hard."

"It doesn't have to be any harder than you're making it," I said. "Talk to me."

"Max asked me to marry him," she said, the words tumbling out of her as though she were afraid that if she didn't say them quickly enough, she'd never be able to.

"*My* Max?" I asked, immediately regretting my choice of words.

Emily frowned a little as she replied, "Honestly, I like to think of him as *my* Max now."

"Of course he is," I answered quickly. I'd been married to Max years ago, and he'd done such a good job convincing me that he would be a better husband than he was an actor that I'd grown to call him The Great Impersonator after our time together was over. "What did you say?"

"I said yes," she answered, and at that moment, I could see her happiness spilling out over her dread. "It makes me a pretty lousy friend, doesn't it?"

"Emily, he wasn't right for me. Maybe he'll be right for you," I said.

"Suzanne, you set us up, remember? If you hadn't come to me and pled his case, I *never* would have gone out with him again."

"Hang on a second. Don't blame that on me," I said.

"I wasn't *blaming* you," she answered curtly.

"I know that. I didn't mean it that way." I took a deep breath and tried to buy a little time so I could wrap my head around the idea of Max marrying Emily. No, I just couldn't do it. It was going to take some time before I could do that. In the meantime, I didn't want to alienate my good friend. "What it all boils down to is that if you're happy, then I'm happy for you."

"I *knew* you'd understand," she said as she leaned over the table and hugged me. "That makes my next question so much easier to ask."

"Would you like me to cater your wedding with donuts?" I asked a little too flippantly.

If she'd caught my tone of voice, she didn't let on. "What a wonderful idea! Why didn't I think of that? Of course I'll have you cater it. Do you think you'll be able to do that, too?"

"What do you mean, too?" I asked her.

"Since you're the one who's responsible for getting us together, it's only fitting that you be my maid of honor."

I couldn't help it. My jaw nearly hit the ground. "Surely there's someone else who might be a more appropriate choice. How about friends you had growing up?"

"We've all drifted apart," she said. "I understand if you say no, but it would mean a great deal to me if you'd say yes."

I had to stall a little. "Have you run this idea past

Max?" Surely my ex would get me out of this jam. I couldn't imagine he'd be all that interested in seeing me walk down the aisle ahead of his new bride. It had to be too much of a déjà vu experience for him to even entertain.

"Are you kidding? He thought it sounded wonderful," Emily said, that smile resurfacing in all of its glory again.

"You really do love him, don't you? Emily, I hate to ask this, but isn't this all kind of sudden? After all, you haven't been dating that long." I'd been with Jake a lot longer than she'd been with Max, and we hadn't even discussed the possibility of getting married. My boyfriend had lost his first family in a car accident, and I knew that it had taken nearly everything he'd had to let me into his life.

"How long do you need, when you know that it's going to last forever?" Emily asked me.

"And you're sure you want me in your wedding party," I said. "It's not too late to change your mind."

"I can't think of anyone else I'd rather have standing up with me than you," she said. Were those tears tracking down her cheeks into her smile? That just wasn't fair. How could I possibly say no to that?

"Okay, if you're sure it's what you really want," I said.

"This is wonderful," Emily said as she stood quickly. "I can't thank you enough. We've got a lot of work ahead of us. The wedding is in three days."

"Three days! Why the rush?" I asked, standing as well. And then I thought of the one reason there might be urgency to the pending nuptials. "Emily, you're not…" I just couldn't seem to bring myself to finish asking that particular question.

"What? No, of course not. I just don't see any reason to wait. I want to be his wife *right now*, Suzanne. Don't worry about the details. Mom has already said that she's willing to pitch in, and Dad's been saving for this for years."

"Then I suppose we'd better get started," I said as I looked at my watch. "I've got another fifteen minutes until I close the donut shop. Why don't we grab lunch at the Boxcar and talk about it there?"

"That sounds perfect," she said. "There's just one more thing. Max insists that his old college roommate be his best man. I hope that won't be a problem."

"You're not talking about *Peter*, are you?" Peter Hickman was the last person in the world I ever wanted to see again, let alone be with in the wedding party. While I knew that most of Max's sins over the years had been committed out of sheer thoughtlessness, Peter could be malicious in *his* motivations. He'd been the best man at our wedding, too, and I still woke up in horror sometimes in the middle of the night reliving his drunken speech at the rehearsal dinner.

"He's changed, too, Suzanne. Just you wait. You'll see." Emily frowned for a moment, and then she said, "I really must be going. There are a million things I have to do. I'm so glad that you're going to be a part of it all. Do me a favor, would you? If you'd keep this quiet for now, I'd appreciate it."

"How long do you need?" I asked. "I hate to keep anything from Momma or Jake."

"I need an hour, and then you can tell whoever you'd like to about it. I'll see you soon at the Boxcar."

"Bye," I said. As I walked back into the donut shop, I wondered what I'd gotten myself into. It was too late to back out now though, even if I wanted to.

It appeared that I was not only going to be present, but I was also going to be a part of my ex-husband's wedding.

If I'd known that morning what was going to happen that day, I wouldn't have gotten out of bed, but it was too late for that now.

Apparently I had a wedding to plan and cater, and just

a few days to do it.

Ten minutes after Emily was gone, a man I hadn't seen in ages came into the donut shop.

"Hey, Jude," I said, trying not to smile. I wasn't a big fan of Gabby Williams's nephew, but I couldn't help myself from repeating the Beatles song every I saw him. We'd gone to high school together, but we'd never been all that close. Jude had been a bit of a bully back then, and I hadn't seen anything over the intervening years to show me that he'd changed. He and Max had been close for years, but in the past several months I heard that they'd had a falling out, which just proved to me yet again how much my ex had changed for the better. I especially wasn't thrilled to see Jude because Emily had gone out with him for awhile six months earlier before she'd gotten tired of his antics. When she'd dumped him, he hadn't taken it well at all.

"Hey," he said gruffly. He wasn't a fan of the greeting, but what could he do? It was his name, after all. "Give me three glazed and a coffee to go."

"What brings you back to town?" I asked him as I got him his order. I knew that he and his aunt had a tumultuous relationship. When his folks had died, Gabby had taken him in at sixteen. He'd left on his eighteenth birthday, but he still came back to April Springs on occasion.

"Are you kidding? There's no place else I'd rather be," he said, but his grin told me that he was up to something. "I heard a rumor that something was going to be happening here, and I wouldn't miss it for the world." I wondered how Gabby felt about him just showing up?

After he got his change and his order, he left without another word. Trouble usually followed him around.

I hoped that this time things would be different, but I wasn't counting on it.

Chapter 3

"There she is, Little Miss Sunshine herself," I heard an old familiar voice say as he walked in the door of Donut Hearts three minutes before we were supposed to close for the day. Why hadn't I locked the doors when I'd had the chance?

"Hello, Peter." At least there was a counter between us. Blast it all, he was even more handsome than he'd been the last time I'd seen him. If there were any justice in the world, his exterior would reflect his rotten interior, but no such luck.

"How about a kiss?" he asked loudly, causing my last three customers of the day to stare at me as though I'd suddenly sprouted horns.

"I'm not even sure that I want to shake your hand," I said.

He laughed at my comment, though I hadn't meant it to be a joke. "It's good to know that some things don't change. You still have that charming sense of humor of yours. What do you say the best man and the maid of honor spend a little time getting reacquainted?"

"I wouldn't be interested even if I *weren't* seeing a state trooper," I said.

Peter smiled, but there wasn't much warmth in it. "Is he stationed around here?"

"No, he's a special investigator, so he goes wherever he's needed."

"Good for him," Peter said, the relief obvious in his voice. Had he been serious about trying to strike something up with me? The man had to be madder than a hatter if he thought there was a chance of that happening. "Still, I hope you'll save at least one dance for me at the reception."

"I wouldn't count on it," I said.

Emma came out of the back just then, and her gaze

took Peter in immediately. She usually didn't go for older men, and I wanted to make sure that she didn't start now. "Hello," she said tentatively.

"Suzanne, why on earth would you keep someone so beautiful in back? Is it so she doesn't outshine the customers? They must all be drab and dull compared to her."

Emma actually blushed at the lame compliment. "Thanks," she said as she tucked a few errant strands of hair behind her ear.

"Aren't you going to introduce us, Suzanne?" Peter asked, his attention never leaving Emma for a single moment.

"Emma, this is Peter. Peter, meet Emma."

He reached for her hand, and then he started to actually kiss it. I stepped in between them at the last second, breaking Peter's focus. "Emma, let's start getting everything ready to close."

"I'm on it," she said, still looking back at Peter as she walked through the kitchen door.

I leaned over the counter after she was gone and said in a harsh whisper, "That girl is off limits. Do you understand me? She's not just an employee; she's a dear friend of mine. If you so much as glance in her direction again, I'll make sure that you live to regret it."

Perhaps I hadn't spoken as softly as I'd meant to, because as I finished, Nancy Patton drew a loud breath and scurried out of the donut shop. Close on her heels were the other two remaining customers, strangers who happened to pick a bad day for a first-time visit.

"My goodness, why all of the open hostility, Suzanne?" Peter asked when we were alone.

"Do you even *remember* your wedding toast?" I asked him, trying my best to fight back my anger.

He hung his head low. "I'm truly sorry about that. It was disgraceful. I apologize. I lost control of myself that night."

"Yes, you did," I said. I needed to take a deep breath. After all, if I could forgive Max for cheating on me and ruining our marriage, why couldn't I forgive Peter for toasting our send-off maliciously? "Let's start over. Emily tells me that you've changed, and I'm going to give you the benefit of the doubt and believe that she's right, until you prove me wrong." I stuck out my hand, and he took it.

"Thank you. I'll try not to disappoint you."

"I'd appreciate that," I said. "But I meant what I said about Emma. She may *look* like a full-grown woman, but she's still got some growing up to do, and she doesn't need any help from you."

"I'll steer clear of her," he said.

I could only hope that he was telling the truth.

Emma popped out of the kitchen, her apron now off and her makeup freshened. Apparently this was going to be harder than I thought. She said, "Peter, I'm getting off work, and if you'd like someone to show you around town, I'd be delighted to do it."

He glanced quickly at me before he spoke, and then Peter said, "I appreciate the offer, Emma, but I'm afraid I'm going to be tied up. Besides, I've been here before, though it was a long time ago."

Emma couldn't hide her disappointment, and I felt a little guilty about it, but better to be a little hurt right now than devastated later. It probably wasn't my place to interfere, but I hadn't been able to help myself. Just when I thought that I'd actually been making progress in my quest to grow up myself, I managed to find a way to act otherwise. The funny thing was that I would have done exactly the same thing all over again, given the chance. I'd meant what I'd said. Emma was my friend, and if I could spare her some pain, I'd do it.

"That's fine. I understand," she said, and then she turned to me. "Everything's taken care of in back. If you'd like, I can do the last two trays."

"I've got it covered. Go on, take off," I said with a smile.

"Thanks, Suzanne. I'll see you tomorrow."

Emma nodded curtly to Peter, and then she left.

"You really do care about her, don't you?" Peter asked me softly.

"I do. She and Emily are two of my very best friends, along with Grace and Trish, of course."

"How is Grace these days?" he asked.

I didn't have to warn him about paying too much attention to her. Grace would be able to handle him with no problem at all. In fact, I kind of *hoped* he made a play for her at the wedding. It would be a real pleasure watching her dismantle him right in front of me.

"She's doing quite well, as a matter of fact," I said.

"Married, I suppose," Peter said.

"No."

"Really?" he asked, a hint of interest slipping into his voice.

"Really and truly. Now if you'll excuse me, I have a business to close."

Peter nodded as he looked around. "Max told me about this when you bought it. You've done quite well for yourself, haven't you?"

"I'm happy," I said, and I realized that now, more than ever, it was true. Sure, I would have loved having more customers, and seeing Jake stationed closer to April Springs would have been nice, but I *liked* living in my childhood home with my mother. We'd grown to be more than mother and daughter since I'd come to live with her after my disastrous divorce from Max. Actually, I should thank him at the wedding. If he hadn't cheated on me, I never would have gotten to know my mother as a person and not just as an authority figure from my past, not that she *still* didn't order me around now and then.

"That's good to hear. Now, if you'll excuse me, I've

got some plans of my own to make."

"Don't tell me that you're involved in the wedding planning, too," I said. Was I going to have to spend every bit of the next three days with *him*?

"No, I have a more important task than that. I'm in charge of the bachelor party again." That grin resurfaced, and I wondered just how much the man had changed after all.

Only time would tell, and I was fresh out of that at the moment.

I was balancing my register when my cellphone rang. I nearly ignored it since I was going to be late as it was, but when I saw who was calling me, that didn't seem to matter anymore.

"Jake, I miss you!" I said.

"Sorry I've been gone so much lately," he said, his voice heavy with weariness. We'd been dating for a while now, and I could tell that something was weighing heavily upon him.

"Are you okay? How's the case going?" He was working on a double homicide, a pair of newlyweds as a matter of fact. Someone had robbed them on their honeymoon, and then shot them as well. It was dark business, and I didn't know how he stood it all of the time.

"It's over. We caught the guy. Turns out that he went off his meds and just went crazy. The Bannisters just happened to be at the wrong place at the wrong time. I don't want to talk about it, if it's all the same to you."

"I understand completely. So, when am I going to see you again?" I asked cheerfully.

"I've got tomorrow off, so I'm headed your way right now, if that's okay with you."

I couldn't help myself; I whooped into the phone.

"It's more than okay, mister. I can't *wait* to see you."

"Me, too, you," he said so softly that I could barely

make out his words. "Suzanne, will we have some time to talk?"

"That sounds ominous," I said. "Did you have any topic in particular in mind?"

Jake sighed heavily, and then he said, "It's too complicated to get into over the phone. I'll be there in six hours."

I knew better than to push him about it, no matter how much my curiosity was aroused. "I'll see you then. We can go to Napoli's tonight."

"If it's all the same to you, I'd rather not go out. Could we eat at your place?"

"If you don't mind leftovers, we're all set," I said.

"That would be fine."

"I'll see you soon," I said. "I love you," I added softly.

"Me, too," he said, and then he hung up.

What was that all about? Was I about to be *dumped*? I couldn't imagine what would make Jake decide not to be with me anymore. If I let myself dwell on it, I'd be in tears by the time he made it into town. I'd hear what he had to say when he got here, but in the meantime, I had a job to do.

It was going to be difficult *before* he'd called me, though.

Now it felt as though it was going to be close to impossible, but I'd find a way.

For Emily.

"Hey, Trish," I said as I walked into the crowded Boxcar Grill. I might have made a mistake choosing it for my wedding planning meeting with Emily. Not only was seating at a premium, but the quarters were awfully close as well. It wouldn't take long for everyone there to figure out what we were doing.

"Hi, Suzanne," she said as I turned around to leave. "Was it something I said?" Trish asked as she followed me out of the diner.

"No, it's just a little too crowded for my taste right now," I answered.

"Don't worry. I can find you a place to sit. Come on back inside."

"It's not that important," I said.

"You are one of my very best friends. There's *always* a place for you."

"It's not just the crowd," I said as a few folks walked past us into the diner. We were garnering more attention than I liked just standing there. It was one of the perils of living in a small town. "Truthfully, I need to have a private conversation."

"With me?" Trish asked as a frown crossed her face. "What happened?"

"Trish, it's got nothing to do with you," I said as I smiled at my friend. "It involves Emily Hargraves."

"What did *she* do?" Trish asked with a grin.

"Nothing bad," I said, and then I added, "At least I don't think so. I hope not, anyway."

"Suzanne, if you're trying to be cryptic, you're doing a bang-up job."

"Normally I'd be happy to share the news with you, but I've been sworn to secrecy."

Trish's grin broadened. "Now you're just trying to kill me with suspense, aren't you?"

The diner door opened, and our mayor, George Morris, came out. "Trish, will you ring me up, or is this meal on the house?"

"Mayor, I don't give away free food, not even to local dignitaries."

"Then will you at least take my money?" George asked. "I'm late for a city council meeting."

"I didn't think you liked those meetings anyway," I said.

He grinned. "I don't, but I'll be dipped in tar if I'm going to let *them* off the hook. If I don't show up, it turns into the seventh grade all over again."

"Give me your money and I'll bring you your change later," Trish said. "Suzanne and I are having a little chat."

As she said it, Emily walked up and joined us. She frowned at me as she asked, "What are you all talking about?"

Was she afraid that I'd spilled the beans about her wedding already? I had to nip that quickly. "The mayor was just telling us about the city council."

"I see," Emily said. "Suzanne, sorry I'm late. Shall we go on in?"

"Actually, it's pretty crowded in there," I said, trying to warn Emily that our conversation wouldn't be all that private if we ate inside. "It will be hard not to be overheard by the people around us."

She frowned, and then smiled suddenly. "That's okay. I'm ready to tell the world now."

"Tell them what?" George asked.

"I'm getting married," Emily said proudly.

"Congratulations," the mayor said, and then he surprised us all by kissing her on the cheek. "Good luck to you."

"Thank you," she answered.

Trish looked at Emily askance, but she refrained from saying anything more than offering her own congratulations. "Come on, Mayor. Let's ring you up," she said as she put her arm in George's. She paused on the steps and turned back to us. "Are you two coming?"

"Why not?" I asked. "Lead the way."

Chapter 4

Fortunately, not many diners took much notice of Emily and me as we walked in. There was a booth free near the back, though the table was still dirty. I saw Gabby Williams sitting next to it, and I knew that we were in for trouble. Gabby ran ReNEWed, the gently used clothing store beside my donut shop. I wasn't at all sure that you could call our relationship a love/hate one, but it was on tenuous grounds most of the time. "Do you happen to know if this table is free?" I asked Gabby as I pointed to the table.

"Nothing here is *free*, but nobody's sitting at that booth," she said.

"Good enough," I answered. "Jude came by my shop this morning."

Gabby didn't answer, unless you counted her disinterested shrug as one. Okay, I didn't need to talk about her nephew if she didn't. I told Emily, "Why don't you sit down. I'll be right back." I grabbed a large black tub used for collecting dirty dishes and started cleaning off our table. I was still searching for a rag to wipe it down when Trish showed up.

"You don't have to do that, Suzanne."

"I don't mind," I said as she took the tub from me.

"Just for that, you get a ten percent employee discount today," Trish said with a smile.

Jack Jefferson said, "I refilled my tea glass. Do I get one, too?"

"Jack, I should charge you more," she said with a smile.

"Why?"

"Because I can," she replied with a grin. After Trish wiped the table down, I took a seat across from Emily.

"Now, I'll be honest with you. I don't even know where to get started," I said.

"It won't be that bad, I promise. Mom's taking care of the venue and the food afterwards, Max reserved the Senior Center stage for the venue, and he's having the rehearsal dinner catered. You're doing the wedding donuts, so really, all that leaves are a few details here and there. It'll be over in a snap."

"Are you sure about having donuts served at your wedding?" I asked her. "Goodness knows that I love them myself, but it's kind of unconventional, wouldn't you say?"

"We passed that exit a long time ago when you agreed to be my maid of honor," Emily said with a smile. "Not many women would agree to serve such a vital role at their ex's wedding."

"What can I say? It's taken me some time, but Max and I have come a long way since the bad old days."

"I'm in awe of that, if you want to know the truth," Emily said.

"Don't give me too much credit," I said with a slight grin. "I'm human enough, and if you don't believe me, just ask Jake."

"He's coming to the wedding too, of course," Emily said.

"If he can get away," I replied, intentionally leaving it a bit vague. Hopefully Emily wouldn't ask me anything else about my current boyfriend.

She must have seen something in my expression, though. "Suzanne, is everything all right?"

"It's fine," I said, not wanting *any* of her focus on me. This was Emily's time to shine, and I was going to make sure that I didn't do anything to spoil that. "What do your three buddies think about all of this?" I wasn't talking about her real friends, though the three stuffed animals that had played such a vital role in her childhood were still near and dear to her. She had them perched on a shelf at her store, and we all loved to see how she was going to outfit them next.

"Spots is excited, Cow isn't quite sure about it, and Moose is being his usual inscrutable self."

"Are they going to attend the wedding?" I asked her.

"You bet. I've been working on tuxes for all three of them since Max proposed. They are all going to be quite dashing."

"I'm certain that they will be," I said. "Now, let's get down to the details."

Trish came by and we both ordered lunch, but it didn't even break our rhythm. By the time we were ready to leave, we'd ironed everything out. Besides the donut wedding treats, I was in charge of getting the reverend to agree to perform the ceremony, and I had the added dubious task of keeping Peter from drinking too much at the rehearsal dinner and the reception the next day. How I was going to do that was anybody's clue.

I insisted on treating Emily to lunch, and sure enough, Trish gave me the employee discount. "You're crazy. You know that, don't you?" I asked her with a grin.

"I know good help when I see it. Anytime you want to moonlight, come to me."

"I might have to take you up on that someday," I replied.

"You don't even have to ask," Trish said.

Emily and I were standing outside when Max rushed up to us.

"Hello, darling," Emily said, and her face truly did light up when she saw him.

Max's expression was more one of concern. "Hi, Em. Have you seen Peter, by any chance?"

"No, I haven't," Emily said.

"I have," I piped up. "He was at the donut shop a little before eleven."

"Then it appears that you were the last person to see him," Max said. "I'm getting worried about him. It's not like him to just disappear, and to top things off, I just heard that Jude was back in town."

"He came by the shop, too," I said.

"What did he want?" Emily asked me. She was clearly upset learning that he'd resurfaced.

"He wouldn't say." I turned to Max. "Why are you so concerned about Peter's whereabouts?"

"We were supposed to get together twenty minutes ago, but he never showed up. He promised me that he wouldn't pull any stunts this week, and now he misses our first rendezvous time."

Emily touched his shoulder lightly. "Don't worry, dear. I'm sure that he'll turn up soon."

"I hope so," Max said. "I'd hate for anything to ruin our wedding."

She put her arms on his shoulders and looked straight into his eyes. "It won't. Nothing will. Everything is going to be perfect."

Max appeared to take great comfort in that, and I was amazed by the changes that had taken place in him over the past six months. He'd grown up a great deal, and he and Emily were clearly in love.

I just hoped that Emily was right, and that nothing would ruin the start of their new life together.

After Max and Emily took off in search of Peter, I decided that I had time to go home and take a shower before Jake showed up. His tone of voice when we'd spoken earlier on the phone had been dire, but I couldn't let it get to me yet. If the news were indeed bad, I'd deal with it when I heard it, but I was going to do my best not to borrow trouble in the meantime. If I was lucky, Momma would be out taking care of one of her many businesses and I wouldn't have to tell her what had happened. It wasn't that I didn't enjoy talking to her, but a part of me felt that if I put my fears into words, they had a better chance of happening. I knew that was ridiculous on the face of it, but that still didn't make it any easier.

"Hello, Suzanne," Momma said as I walked into the living room of the small cottage we shared on the edge of the park.

"Where's your car?" I asked her as I shut the door behind me. When I'd driven up in my Jeep, I had felt a wave of relief sweep over me to find the driveway empty.

And yet here she was.

"It's in the shop," she said. "The tow truck driver was kind enough to run me home when I had troubles with it. Wasn't that sweet of him?"

"He must be a real doll," I said. "Aren't you going to need your car, though?"

"I'll have it back in an hour. I've been promised," she said. After carefully studying me, Momma asked softly, "Suzanne, are you okay?"

"I'm fine. Why wouldn't I be? Emily and Max are getting married in three days, and I'm their maid of honor." I didn't want to talk about Jake, so what better way to distract my mother than by bringing up the other jarring news about my life?

"You actually *agreed* to that?" Momma asked. "What were you thinking?"

"That I couldn't refuse a friend's request," I said simply enough. "I honestly believe that Max has changed, and it was important to Emily that I do this, so I agreed."

Momma nodded, and then she added a slight grin. "Suzanne, you have to admit, it *is* a bit unconventional."

"When have *we* ever been conventional?" I asked, matching her smile with one of my own.

"That's a fair point. I just can't believe you'd take this on."

"Hold on. It gets better. I'm also making a donut display for the wedding. They've decided to have my treats instead of a wedding cake."

"I can't disagree with that," she said. Though she was a diminutive woman in size, my mother more than made up for it with the sheer size of her personality. "Are her little stuffed friends going to be in the wedding party?"

"I'm pretty sure that she wouldn't get married without them," I said. "She's going to make tuxedos for all three of them."

Momma's grin got even bigger. "I can't wait to see that. It's almost worth the cost of admission in and of itself. I wonder what Max will think about that?"

"He loves Emily, and that means that he's bought into the idea from the start that Cow, Spots, and Moose are as real and as animated as we are."

"It sounds as though he really *has* changed," Momma said.

"I never would have pled his case to Emily in the first place if I hadn't believed it," I said.

"So, once again, no good deed goes unpunished. As a reward for your kindness, you'll have the privilege of walking down the aisle just ahead of Emily, and Max will see your face just before he sees his betrothed. What does Jake think about all of this?"

"As a matter of fact, I haven't told him yet," I said, averting my gaze.

"Don't you think it's something that he'll want to know?" she asked. I knew that slightly scolding tone of voice too well.

"This all just happened," I said. "Jake's on his way here, and if I get the opportunity to bring it up, I will, but I have a hunch that he's got something more serious on his mind. He told me that we needed to talk." As soon as I said the last bit, I wanted to clamp my jaws shut, but it was too late. I'd let my frustration with Jake's mystery cloud my ability to watch what I said around my mother.

"That doesn't sound too promising," Momma said. "What do you think he wants to talk about?"

"I think he might be dumping me," I said, shocking myself even more than Momma. Why in the world was I still talking?

"He knows better than to throw you back," Momma said dismissively. "You are a jewel of a woman, and he'd be lucky to have you."

"But what if he doesn't want me anymore?" I asked. I was on the edge of tears, but I fought them with everything I had. I knew that if I started crying, Momma would not be far behind, and then we'd both be a mess. If my worst fears were realized, there would be plenty of time for tears later.

"Have you considered the other possibility?" she asked.

"What's that?"

"What if he's about to propose?" she asked. "You said he sounded serious. It might be something good instead of bad."

"I don't think so," I said.

"But you don't know, do you?"

"No, but I've got a pretty good idea," I said.

"Well, there's nothing you can do until he gets here. I'll make myself scarce even if I have to walk over to the Boxcar. That way, I'll be close by if you need me."

"You don't have to leave the cottage on my account," I said, though it was my most fervent wish at the moment.

"You are my daughter, and I love you," she said simply as she stood and kissed my forehead. "I know you love your shower, but why don't you take some time for yourself and have a nice long soak in the tub, instead? It will do wonders for you; I guarantee it."

"Maybe I will," I said. I kissed her cheek and hugged her. "Thanks for being here for me."

"There's nowhere else that I'd rather be," she said. "You smell just like donuts; you know that, don't you?"

"It's hard not to after making them and then serving them all morning," I said as I started to pull away.

She wouldn't let me, though. "I wasn't complaining," she said. "It's really rather quite nice. They should make a fragrance of it."

"Grace's cosmetics company tried that," I said. "We both got nice little checks for the idea, but nothing ever came of it."

"It's just as well," Momma said as she released me. "The men would never leave you alone."

"I have a feeling that they'd find a way," I said. "I'm going to go take that bath now, if you don't mind."

"You do that, and I'll walk over to the diner."

"You don't have to leave right now," I said as I glanced at the clock. "You've got at least an hour still."

"I'd rather be safe than sorry," she said. "Good luck, and call me after he leaves, no matter what."

"I will," I said. "I promise."

After Momma was gone, I drew a bath, something I rarely did these days. As the tub filled, I turned the ringer off my cellphone, put it in my bedroom to charge, and then I shut the door. I wouldn't be able to hear the house landline phone from in there, either.

All I needed at the moment was a little quiet time just for me.

Chapter 5

I don't know how it happened, but I must have dozed off in the tub, because when I woke up with a start, I realized that it was past my allotted hour to soak. The water was cold, and I had a stiff neck; so much for my relaxing bath. Any good that it had done was long gone. I drained the water, showered off quickly, and then dried off, put on my robe, and walked into my bedroom.

My cellphone had a message stored on it. Had Jake called me while I'd been asleep? I entered my code and listened to my message. Sure enough, his voice came on the line. "Hey, it's me. I've been called back to the office for an important meeting with my boss. It looks as though I won't be able to make it tonight after all. Don't try to call; I'm turning my ringer off. It's pointless anyway, as this sounds as though it's going to be a late night, and don't forget, you have to get up early tomorrow morning. We'll talk as soon as we can, but I can't say right now when exactly that will be. Sorry about the drama and confusion. I'll explain it all the next time we talk. Bye. Oh, love ya. Bye again."

The love he'd sent my way had been cooler than the bathwater when I'd climbed out of the tub. It meant either one of two things; he was already preoccupied with another case, or his feelings for me were beginning to cool as well. I didn't know which one it might be, and I had no way of finding out now, either.

I was still staring at my phone when it rang. I searched the caller ID, but unfortunately, it was the imminent bride and not my boyfriend.

Trying my best to sound chipper, I said, "Hey, Emily. Any sign of the missing best man yet?"

"He showed up three minutes ago," Emily said. "He's got a black eye, and the knuckles on his right hand are bruised. I don't know what happened, but Max is pushing him for the details right now."

"Who could he have gotten into a fight with in April Springs? Does he even *know* anybody here but the three of us?"

"I don't even want to think about that right now," she said. "Mom called, and she needs to see us both immediately. Can you drop everything you had planned tonight and come over to her place?"

"Why not? I've got nothing going on," I said, although it pained me to admit it to her.

"That's perfect. I hope you haven't eaten yet; Mom's made a feast. Oh, I have one more favor to ask of you, if you don't mind."

"Hey, I'm the maid of honor. I live to serve you," I replied.

She laughed at my attempt at humor. "We both know better than that, but would you mind swinging by and picking up Grace?"

"Is she in the wedding, too?" I asked.

"She and Emma both," Emily answered.

"Are there going to be enough matching groomsmen to go around?" I asked. Max wasn't known for longevity in his friendships, with the possible exception of Peter, and that was one that I wished hadn't stuck all those years.

"He's asked a few actors that he's worked closely with before."

"How festive," I said.

"Emma's already here, but it would be great if you could give Grace a lift."

"We're on our way," I said, and I hung up before she could give me any more assignments.

"Well, if it's not the bravest woman in all of April Springs, North Carolina," Grace said after I pulled up in front of her house just down the street from the cottage that I shared with Momma.

"Why do you say that?" I asked as she climbed into my Jeep.

"You're the maid of honor at your ex-husband's wedding," she said. "And you don't think that's brave? I think you should get a medal for doing this."

"I'm doing it for Emily," I said.

"There's absolutely no doubt in my mind that's true," she answered.

"I didn't realize that you were going to be in the wedding party, too," I said.

"Emily and I are pals, too," she said. "I'm surprised Emma's not in it, though."

"She's already there," I said as I drove to Emily's place.

"To be honest with you, I'm a little surprised that *she's* not the maid of honor," Grace said, "not that you won't make a perfectly lovely one."

"It turns out that I was asked because I persuaded Emily to give Max another try."

She grinned at me. "Oh, boy, I'm willing to bet that you're regretting that now."

"You know me too well," I said as we neared Emily's parents' house.

"Suzanne, are you okay?" What was it with Momma, and now Grace? Was I giving out some kind of signal that I was in desperate straits?

"I'm fine," I said.

"Really?"

"No, I'm a train wreck waiting to happen, but I don't want to talk about it right now. How about if we table it until after we leave tonight? Would you do that for me?"

"I will," she said, and then she squeezed my hand. "Whatever it is, I'm here for you, okay?"

"I know," I said as I squeezed her hand back. "Now, let's go see what we can do to make the bride's life a little easier, shall we?"

"Sounds great to me," Grace said. I noticed her watching me closely, searching for some kind of sign of what was really wrong with me, but I wasn't about to tell her now. This was Emily's time, and I was going to do my best to help make her shine.

At least I had my early hours as an excuse to get out of there. It had all turned out to have been one big false alarm, a pretense to gather us all together so we could see how thoroughly we'd been replaced by Emily's mother.

"Thanks for being my ride," Grace said as we headed back home.

"You're welcome. I was glad to do it."

"Oh, I appreciate the lift," Grace said with a smile, "but what I really loved was the excuse to get out of there early. Don't get me wrong. I love Emily to death, but I thought that her mother would *never* shut up. Do you feel left out?"

"How do you mean?"

"Suzanne, she took over every single one of your duties, including lining up the reverend. Can you believe that binder she had? It must have weighed twenty pounds. I'll bet she's been working on it since Emily was a little girl. Who knows, maybe even longer. There's literally nothing left for you to do."

"Are you kidding? I just have to make the wedding donuts and show up. That sounds perfect to me," I said.

"If you're sure," Grace said. She paused a moment, and then my best friend asked me, "Will you tell me what's going on now?"

As I pulled up into her driveway, I said, "I'll make you a deal. I'll tell you, but you can't ask me any questions or make any comments. When I'm finished, we say good night. Agreed?"

"Agreed," she said. Wow, she really *did* want to know what was going on with me to agree to those terms.

"Jake was on his way here to discuss something serious with me when he was called back to his office suddenly. I have a feeling that he's about to break up with me." I managed to say it all without crying, which was a big deal for me, given how I felt about the situation.

Grace had a look of pure shock on her face, as though I'd stunned her into silence. After a slight pause, she held up one finger, and her expression begged me for the chance to say one thing.

"Okay," I relented. "You can say one thing, but that's it."

"I'm here if you need me," Grace said, and then she gave me a hug before she got out of the car.

It was the perfect thing to say.

Now I had just one more gauntlet to run before I could get to sleep, but it would be the toughest one yet. I knew that there was no way that Momma would agree to one comment. No matter what happened, I was in for a long night when I could barely afford to give up the sleep I might still manage before I had to get up and make the donuts yet again.

But Momma was gone when I drove the short way home, though her car was back in its rightful place. She must have been out with Chief Martin, which was fine with me. I crawled into bed at 8:30, turned off my ringer, and fell asleep from sheer exhaustion, both physical and emotional. I decided to be like Scarlett and worry about it tomorrow.

For now, I desperately needed some sleep.

When I woke up the next morning around one, I quietly got dressed and headed downstairs. To my surprise, the kitchen light was on. Had Momma forgotten to turn it off when she'd got in?

Then I smelled the bacon.

"What's this?" I asked as I walked in to find a plate with waffles and bacon at my seat.

"I decided to get up and make you breakfast," Momma said. How did she manage to look so chipper when I knew that she'd gotten in after me?

"I appreciate the thought, but I don't have time," I said.

"You have five minutes to eat, and you know it," she said. "Sit, young lady."

I was about to protest when I took a deep breath. It really did smell wonderful. "Okay. Thanks for this, but let's not make it a regular thing, okay? It's hard enough keeping my weight down making the treats I create every single day. If I start eating breakfasts like this, I won't be able to fit into my Jeep."

"Agreed, for special occasions only," she said with a smile.

As I dove into the breakfast, Momma asked, "Do you have any interest in continuing our discussion we started yesterday?"

I swallowed a bite of waffle, and then I replied, "Mom, I really, really don't. Is that okay with you?"

"It's fine. I'm here for you, though."

"I know, and I appreciate it," I said as I patted her hand. I took one last bite of waffle, added a bit of bacon, and then I savored it. "This was great, but I have to run." I looked around the kitchen and saw how much work she'd put into making me breakfast. "I suppose I could stick around and help you clean up."

"I'm happy to do it. Go on; go make your donuts. The people of April Springs are counting on you."

"Well, maybe a few of them," I said as I kissed her cheek. "Thanks again, for everything."

"What else are mothers for?" she asked with the hint of a smile.

"More than I can say."

As I drove to Donut Hearts in the darkness, I was

thankful again that I'd had a place to come home to after my divorce from Max. I'd been in bad shape, the victim of my husband's affair, and Momma had helped put me back together again. Sure, I'd put on a brave face to the rest of the world, buying the donut shop on an impulse with my divorce settlement, but it had taken some time to see life in a positive light again, and if it hadn't been for Momma and Grace, I'm not entirely sure I would have made it. If my life was about to go through another crisis, at least I'd have both women there to help me through whatever came my way. For now, though, I was going to make donuts and try my best to forget about the rest of the world.

As I approached Donut Hearts, I realized that it might be easier said than done.

Chief Martin was waiting for me, leaning against his squad car with a dark expression on his face.

It appeared that my day wasn't going to be quite so normal after all.

Chapter 6

"Why do I have the feeling that you're not here for a cup of coffee?" I asked the chief after I'd parked and gotten out of my Jeep.

"I could use some of that, too," he said, "but you're right. That's not the real reason that I'm here."

"What happened?" A sudden thought occurred to me, and I felt my blood go cold. "Did something happen to Jake?" If he'd been hurt after the last conversation that we'd had, I'd never find a way to get over it.

The police chief looked surprised by my question. "What? No, as far as I know, Jake's fine. Why, what's he been up to lately?"

"Investigating crime, just like you," I said as I unlocked the door. "Come on in. I'll get the coffee started while you bring me up to speed on what's happening."

"That sounds fine with me. I never got a chance to get to sleep last night. After I dropped your mother off at the cottage, I got the call, and I've been working on the case all night."

"What happened?" I asked as I flipped one of the coffee pots on. It was our standard blend, not one of Emma's exotics. I had two very different clienteles for the coffee we served; one liked their coffee strong and plain, while the other appreciated the finer nuances of Emma's blends. The chief was definitely a strong and plain coffee kind of guy.

"There was a murder in town last night," he said solemnly.

I hated the thought of it, but I knew that it was as much a part of life in a small town as it was in any big city. "Who was killed?"

"I don't know if you know the man," the chief said. "He was in town for a visit, as a matter of fact."

"Peter Hickman is dead, isn't he?" I asked, remembering Emily telling me about him getting into a fight the day before.

"No, it was Gabby Williams's nephew, Jude."

"That's even worse," I said.

"What makes you say that?" he asked me.

As I poured him a cup of coffee in a paper cup, I said, "I had a feeling that he was going to crash the wedding. Jude and Emily dated not that long ago, and from what I heard, he had a hard time believing that Max had replaced him in Emily's heart. I don't have to tell you that Max has a temper, so yeah, I'm a little worried about that. Then there's Peter Hickman. He got in a fight yesterday, and I have to wonder if that had anything to do with what happened to Jude."

The chief nodded. "That's some good information you've got there," he said. "I've been able to dig up a little more myself. Would you like to hear it?"

"You're actually going to share with me?" I asked him with a smile.

"I'd be an idiot not to admit that you've helped me out in the past, all unofficially, of course. I'm beginning to respect your judgment, Suzanne. Plus, I heard that you were going to be Emily's maid of honor, so is there any way in the world that you and Grace *aren't* going to be digging into this?"

"I'd be lying if I denied it," I said.

"Then let's see what we can do about cooperating."

I was glad that the police chief was seeing me in a different light, but then again, I had been able to solve a few murders with the help of my friends over the years. It would be nice working together instead of fighting all of the time. How much of that was because of his relationship with my mother I didn't know, nor was I all that sure that I cared. "That sounds great to me."

The chief took a long sip of coffee, and then he said, "Gabby had a public fight with Jude two hours before his body was discovered by the railroad tracks. Someone hit him in the back of the head with an iron bar, by the way. From what we've been able to determine so far, it was most likely between eight PM and midnight, but don't quote me on that."

"Gabby took Jude in when no one else would. I can't believe that she would *ever* kill him," I said.

"Hang on. I'm not jumping to any conclusions right now; I'm just gathering facts."

"What else have you got?" I asked him as I topped off his coffee.

"Well, it turns out that Jude had his share of enemies around town. You know about Reggie Nance, don't you?"

"Debbie's dad? What's he got to do with all of this? He comes in and orders a dozen donuts for his office every week. He's a great guy."

"I agree, but Debbie and her baby died in childbirth, and he's never gotten over it. The man lost his wife to cancer, and then soon after, his daughter and granddaughter, all in the span of three months. It would be too much for anybody to stand."

"What does Jude's murder have to do with any of that?" I asked.

"Who do you think the baby's father was?" the chief asked. "Jude denied it, but Debbie was positive. He rejected her completely, and Reggie believed that she lost the fight in her when Jude turned his back on her. The man doesn't have an alibi for the time of the murder, either, so he's near the top of my list."

"I didn't know about any of this," I said. "I heard something around the edges, but I guess I was so busy trying to keep Max in line that I didn't notice what was going on in town."

"You had your hands full as it was," the chief conceded. "Anyway, that's all that I've got right now. If you hear anything else, let me know, okay?"

"Likewise," I said.

Chief Martin stood and took another drink from his coffee cup. "I'd better get back out there and see what I can come up with."

"Shouldn't you go home and at least *try* to get a little sleep?" I asked.

"I've got a cot at the station I can use later," he said. "Thanks again, for the coffee *and* the cooperation."

"Anytime," I said.

After the police chief was gone, I started my routine, turning on the fryer and getting out my photocopied recipe book. As I started the first round of cake donuts, I began to consider the possibilities of who might have killed Jude Williams and how this was going to impact the impending wedding. I was glad for the quiet, since Emma didn't come in for a little while, but I was no closer to reaching any conclusions than I'd been after I'd heard the news. I hoped that Grace had some free time coming. I could use her help in my investigation.

"Did you hear the news?" Emma Blake asked me as she reported for work a little later. "Gabby's nephew was murdered last night." It wasn't all that unusual for Emma to have information about the current events in April Springs, since her father ran the newspaper.

"I heard," I said as I continued to work on the cake donuts. As far as I was concerned, Emma didn't need to know about my arrangement with Chief Martin. As a matter of fact, it might not be a bad idea for me to keep that particular little tidbit to myself. After all, I doubted the chief would appreciate seeing the fact that he'd spoken with me about the case spread out across the front page of the newspaper.

"Man, news travels fast in a small town, doesn't it?"

"You have no idea. Do you mind setting up the front?" I asked her. "I'm going to drop some donuts."

"I'll take care of it," she said as she beat a hasty

retreat. Our donut dropper was large, clunky, and heavy. It had slipped out of my hands once, and I'd made a conscious decision not to fix the dent in the wall it had made on impact. It was a good reminder just how dangerous donut making could be. It also had the added benefit of ending a conversation with Emma that I didn't particularly want to have. She frequently walked a fine line between being my assistant and being her father's daughter, and she'd crossed it a few times in the past, sharing things with him that I hadn't wanted known. I'd decided after the last incident to be a little more discreet about what I shared with her, and so far, it had worked out just fine. I hated to cut off a friend, but my ability to act freely depended on it. Folks had to feel able to speak with me about murder, and they wouldn't do that if they started reading what they'd told me in the newspaper.

After I dropped the last of the cake donuts, I put the dropper in the sink and called out, "It's all clear, Emma."

She rejoined me promptly and got to work on the first round of dishes. As I pulled the last of the cake donuts from the oil and iced them, I said, "We should try something new. I'm afraid things might be getting a little stale around here. Do you have any ideas?"

"I was hoping you'd ask," she said as she reached in the pocket of her blue jeans and pulled out a tattered piece of paper.

"What's that?" I asked her with a smile.

"It's my list of new ideas," she said. "Here goes. I'll just read them off, and you tell me if anything sounds interesting to you. Mango Sherbet. Apricot Honey. Blueberry Jalapeño. Neapolitan. Ginger Ale and Strawberry. Pineapple Ham."

"Are we still talking about donuts?" I asked. What did she do, sit around and dream these things up? Well, I had nobody to blame but myself. I'd asked.

"Fillings, actually," she said. "For example, we take

two raised donuts, fry them like usual, and then add a little fried pineapple and ham in between. We make a sandwich out of it, like they did with a hamburger patty at the state fair. I'll bet it would be delicious."

"Maybe so, but do we really want to open ourselves up for *more* scorn from the diet-conscious folks?"

"They don't have to come in here, but if they do, you usually offer them *something* they can eat."

It was true that I tried to come up with at least a few recipes that wouldn't spike the glucose levels of my customers, but it hadn't been as easy as I'd hoped. Besides, most of them weren't very good sellers. It turned out that most of the people who came into Donut Hearts wanted some comfort food that actually tasted like it was decadent. If there was a way to do that in a healthy manner, I hadn't found it yet. "Tell you what. Pick out your favorite, and we'll try it soon."

"That's going to be tough to narrow it down," she said.

"Do your best," I said with a grin as I put the last cake donuts on a tray and slid the whole thing onto a rolling rack we used to move the finished donuts up front.

"Okay, but I'm not ready to commit to anything yet."

"Take your time," I said as I flipped the pages of my recipe book to my basic glazed donut dough entry. I could put that one together in my sleep, but I got a lot of reassurance out of the fact that I could read it right out of the book. My copy had been stolen and then burned on my front porch, but fortunately, Emma's mother had made one for herself when she worked in the shop while I'd been away. She'd had a copy that I hadn't known about, and all had been saved. I couldn't very well say no to Emma about trying new things after her mother had safeguarded all of my old recipes, and who knew? Maybe she'd come up with a real winner, though I had no idea how things would turn out, given the list she'd read off to me. After I got all of the ingredients together in the mixer and turned it on, I started doing a little cleanup of my own so I'd be ready for the next phase of donut making. The timer went off, and I removed the mixing paddle and covered the bowl with plastic wrap. While we gave the dough time to rise, Emma and I could take a break of our own.

I only had one caveat this morning, though. "I'd love to go outside for our break, but I don't want to talk about Jude Williams. Is that okay with you?"

She nodded, even though I could tell that she was a little disappointed by my request. "That's fine. Would you like to talk about Emily's wedding instead?"

It wasn't my favorite topic in the world, but I had to give her credit; it was still better than murder. "Sure, why not?"

"Suzanne, you're so lucky to be her maid of honor," Emma said as we walked outside.

"I hated to do it, on your account. Emma, we both know that *you* should be standing up there beside her. After all, the two of you are best friends."

"Don't worry about me," Emma said with a broad smile. "Emily explained it all to me, and who could disagree? If it weren't for you, there wouldn't even *be* a wedding."

"Why does everyone keep saying that? They would have found a way to work it out if it was meant to be, Emma."

"Like you and Jake have?" she asked. I must have flinched at my boyfriend's name, because she quickly asked, "Is there something going on between the two of you? He *is* coming to the wedding, isn't he?"

That was the least of my worries, but I didn't want to go into that with Emma. "It's hard to say at this point. He was coming to April Springs when he was called back to Raleigh at the last second."

"It must be great being with such an important man," she said.

"It has its moments," I said. I had to change the

subject again, and I was beginning to wonder if there was anything safe that Emma and I could talk about these days. "How's your love life?" I asked her.

"You don't want to know," she said with a sigh. "Why is it that boys my age are all still boys? Aren't they growing any men these days?"

I laughed. "Are you having trouble with young men in general, or is there one particular one that's driving you a little crazy?"

"Just in general at the moment," she said. "I'm seriously thinking about going after an older man the next time."

"How old are we talking here?" I asked her, wary of what Peter had said to me the day before.

"I don't know. Maybe two or three years older than I am, anyway. What do you think? Is that *too* old for me?"

"No, that sounds just about perfect to me," I said as the timer went off. It was time to go back inside and prep the donuts again before they were ready for proofing. "No rest for the weary," I said as I stood.

"Or the wicked, either," Emma replied with a grin.

"I'm not exactly sure which we are," I answered in kind.

"Can't we be both?" she asked me.

"Today we can be anything we put our minds to," I replied.

"Then I want to be home in bed," Emma said with a laugh.

"Well, *almost* anything," I replied as we walked in and I locked the door behind us. We had a long few hours of donutmaking before we opened our doors for our first customers, and I for one was ready to get busy making treats. I might not be able to cure any disease or comfort anyone in serious pain, but I still managed to bring out a few smiles in the course of my day, and that was worth something.

afraid of being thrown in jail for her nephew's murder.

"Gabby, I'm sure that nobody thinks you killed Jude."

She laughed with clear scorn. "Suzanne, you're not that naïve. We both know how folks in this town can circle like sharks when they sense blood in the water."

"That's not always true," I said. "There are a *lot* of people who believe in you."

"I wish I could agree with you, but we both know that I don't go out of my way to make close friends. I'm afraid I could count them all on one hand besides you."

I tried to hide my surprise. Did she really consider us close friends? Sure, we usually got along okay, but she'd never been to my home on a social visit, and I'd certainly never been to hers when I didn't have a pressing reason in the past, say murder. "If it means anything, I don't think you killed Jude."

"I appreciate that, but I need more than that from you. I'm desperate. Suzanne, you've got to find his killer."

I was already planning to do just that, but it might not be smart to tell her that. "I'll do what I can."

That's when she smiled for the first time since I'd first seen her that day. "I knew I could count on you. If there's anything that I can do to help you, let me know."

"Well, for starters, you can answer a few questions."

"Fire away."

I had to tread lightly. Gabby had a well-deserved reputation for having a temper, and I'd seen it firsthand myself more than once over the years. "When did you last see Jude?"

"Last night around eight," she said.

"Where were you, at your place?"

She scowled a little. "No, we were in front of the grocery store. I saw him drinking out of a bottle hidden by a brown paper bag, and I scolded him for drinking in public."

"How did he react to that?"

"How do you think? He started ranting and raving

about how he wasn't a kid anymore, and that he could do *what* he wanted *when* he wanted. He also said something that puzzled me at the time."

"What was that?"

Gabby frowned as she explained, "He told me that he'd go wherever he wanted to, and talk to anybody he darn well pleased, and there was nothing that all of April Springs could do about it. I had no idea what he was talking about, and I suspected that he was more than a little drunk."

I'd have to ask the police chief if Jude had been drunk at the time of his murder, and find out the exact level of his intoxication. It might help establish just how vulnerable he'd been to attack. "So, what did you do?"

"I came here to the shop and brooded about it for a few hours, and then I must have fallen asleep at my desk. I went home so we could continue our conversation, but Jude never showed up. I fell asleep on the couch again while I was waiting, and I didn't wake up until Chief Martin knocked on my door. Let me tell you, that's the worst way to wake up that you could imagine." Gabby wrung her hands together a little, and then she said, "We need to wrap this conversation up. I have to go to the funeral home to start making arrangements. What a nightmare that's going to be."

I thought for one second about volunteering to go with her, but I was pretty sure that wouldn't help me find Jude's killer. "Is there someone you can call to go with you?"

"Margaret's on her way," she said, referring to one of her oldest friends. "Is there anything else that I can do to help?"

"I hate to ask, but I need to see his room at your place," I asked softly, waiting for the backlash from my request.

I kept waiting for Gabby to explode, but she surprised me by handing me her keys. "The police chief has already inspected it, so I doubt you'll find anything, but his room was in the attic. You're welcome to dig around in it all that you want."

"He stayed in the attic?" I asked, a little surprised by the arrangement. Attics might be perfectly fine living spaces in most places, but in the South, they tended to be hot and stuffy, suitable for storage and not much else.

"It's not like that," she explained quickly. "When Jude first came to live with me, he wouldn't use the bedroom I gave him, choosing to sleep on the couch downstairs instead. I told him that it wouldn't do, and when I looked for him the next day, I found him sleeping up there. I fixed it up, even added a little portable air conditioner for one of the dormer windows. It was nice, but more importantly, it was as far as he could get away from me and still be in the house." She looked a little wistful at that moment. "He was a tough kid, and he had a stubborn streak a mile wide. Maybe that's why I loved him so much. He was a lot like his aunt Gabby."

I was again on dangerous ground here. I knew that I couldn't agree with her, but I couldn't exactly contradict her, either, at least not with a straight face. "Thanks for trusting me," I said instead.

"Suzanne, there are days when you're about the only person in this town that I *do* trust." She managed a faint smile as she added, "Then again, there are other days when I don't trust you much either."

"I understand that," I said.

"When you're finished searching his room, just leave the keys on the kitchen table. I've got another set of my own."

"Will do," I said as I glanced at my watch. "Well, I'd better get out of here if I'm going to make any headway on what happened to Jude."

"We know what happened to him," Gabby said grimly. "I just want to know who did it."

"Don't you want to know why, too?" I asked.

"Why can come later. For now, I just need to know who was responsible for ending his life. I know that Jude wasn't always smiling and pleasant to be around, but he was the last bit of family that I had left, and I need to make sure that his murder doesn't go unsolved."

"I'll do everything that I can," I said, feeling the weight of the responsibility she was putting on my shoulders.

"Just make sure that your best is good enough," Gabby said.

It felt odd going into Gabby's house without her even if I *was* using a key and I had her permission. The place was much like her shop; everything there was elegant, if slightly used. The entire downstairs had a Victorian parlor feel to it, a style that I wasn't a big fan of myself, but it must have suited her. I headed straight to the attic once I got inside, not wanting to snoop around in Gabby's life at all while I was there. As I climbed the stairs, I wondered just what I might find there.

The place was nice, which was quite a surprise for me. Calling it an attic didn't do the space justice; it was more like a loft, nicely furnished and stylish in its own right. Gabby's touch was everywhere, but she'd clearly allowed Jude some discretion in his decorations. It gave me chills knowing that the man who had stayed there had been alive just the day before, but I tried to bury that knowledge. I was certain that the police chief and his team had done a thorough job of examining the room, but I also knew that it was impossible to find every secret someone might have hidden. I started with the small desk, going through the drawers thoroughly. There was nothing telling there, or in the closet, or even under the bed. I was about to give up when I noticed a book on the nightstand that looked out of place with everything else that I'd expected to see. It was a collection of love sonnets, something that I thought neither Gabby nor her nephew would choose for light reading. I picked it up, turned it spine-side up, and flipped through the pages, hoping something would flutter to the floor.

Nothing did.

I was about to put it back when I opened the front cover to see if there was any identification there. Maybe an inscription or a library stamp would tell me where it had come from, but I couldn't see a thing. On an impulse, I pulled the front flap to one side, and I still almost missed the name written inside.

In a very feminine hand, the name Lisa Grambling was written, along with a date that was less than two weeks old. How had a married woman's book come to be found in a murdered man's bedroom? Was there a connection between them that nobody knew about? I decided to take the book with me and ask Lisa that question myself. If the police chief had found it, I was sure that he would have spoken with her about it by now, so it wasn't as though I was removing a valuable clue. I wasn't even taking something that belonged to Jude, so there was no reason to tell Gabby about it, either.

At least that was how I was going to justify it to myself.

Tucking the book under my arm, I made my way downstairs. Doing as Gabby had asked, I left the keys and headed out the door. Had it locked behind me? I turned to try the knob when I heard a familiar voice behind me.

"Drop whatever it is you just stole, and put your hands up in the air."

Chapter 8

"Not funny," I said as I turned around to see my best friend, Grace, standing there smiling at me. She'd changed out of her suit into a nice pair of jeans and a sporty little blouse. We could wear the exact same clothes, but I knew that they'd look better on her than they would on me. If she hadn't been such a good friend, I might even have been a little jealous about it. "How did you find me?"

"That Jeep of yours isn't exactly inconspicuous," she said. "I took off a little early to help you."

"How did you know that I'd be at Gabby's place?" I asked as we walked off the porch together.

"I didn't. I was driving by and I saw your Jeep. I tried the doorknob, but it was locked, so I was about to knock when I peeked through the glass and saw you coming down the stairs. Sorry if I startled you."

"I knew that you were there all along," I said with a grin.

"Liar," she answered good-naturedly.

"Fine, you got me."

"So, what did you find inside?"

I looked around and noticed that one of Gabby's neighbors was watching us through his blinds. It was Thad Belmont, a gossip worse than any woman in town. He probably thought we were burglarizing the place, and it wouldn't surprise me if he were calling the police even as he watched us. "Let's do this someplace else, shall we?"

"That's fine by me," Grace said. "It's going to be a little unwieldy driving two cars around. Why don't you follow me home? I can drop my car off, and we can take your Jeep."

"Are you sure you don't mind slumming it with me?" I

asked with a smile. Grace got a brand new company car every other year, each model nicer than the last. As she'd climbed the corporate ladder into management, they weren't afraid to show their satisfaction with the job she was doing.

"I'll find a way to tough it out," she said, smiling back at me.

"Good. See you there." I put the book on the passenger seat and followed Grace home. Once she got out and joined me, I handed her the book.

"Thanks anyway, but I never cared much for love sonnets," she said as she tried to hand it back to me.

"I'm not giving it to you," I said as I pulled out of her driveway. "I found it when I searched Jude's room in the attic."

"I can't believe that Gabby let you go through her house."

"She even gave me her keys. She's upset about Jude, but I think she's also worried that Chief Martin might arrest her for his murder."

After I told her about the scene Gabby and Jude had just hours before he'd been killed, Grace's smile faded quickly. "This whole thing must be a nightmare for her. Imagine how tough it must be not to be able to make up with her nephew now."

"She's in some real pain. I was still surprised when she asked me to help her, not that I wasn't going to investigate this, anyway."

"You didn't tell her that, did you?" Grace asked me.

"Of course not. It's not like I'm working for anybody. This is just something I feel compelled to do."

"Is his murder going to affect the wedding?" she asked.

"How could it not? Emily dated Jude not that long ago, and I can't help wondering if his murder had something to do with the upcoming nuptials."

"I hope not," Grace said.

"All I know is that Emily is determined to get married as soon as she can. She says she can't wait to be Max's wife."

"Did you tell her that status was highly overrated?" Grace asked with that wicked little smile of hers.

"No, and you shouldn't, either. It's pretty clear that Max is a different person than the man I married."

"And divorced," she added.

"That's true," I said. I reached over and tapped the book. "You don't know everything about that book yet. Look inside the flyleaf."

Grace did as I asked, and I glanced over to see her eyebrows shoot up. "Lisa Grambling? Seriously?"

"Do you have a hard time believing that she and Jude might have been having an affair?" I asked.

"No, Lisa's always been really flirty, but her husband, Frank, seems like the jealous type to me, and the man's built like a tank. Was Jude really that crazy?"

"There's only one way to find out," I said as I stopped in front of Lisa Grambling's house. "Let's go ask her ourselves."

"This is going to be fun," Grace said happily.

"Take it easy. We're investigating a murder, remember?"

"I know, but it's exciting tracking down a killer, don't you think?"

"Sometimes a little too much," I said as I turned off the ignition and opened my car door. "Let's go see what Lisa has to say about *this*," I added as I took the book from Grace.

"Thanks, but I don't want any of your donuts," Lisa said after she opened the door. She was a curvy woman with lots of sex appeal, and she wasn't afraid who knew it. "I'm on a diet."

"I'm not out peddling donuts door to door," I said with a smile. "I'd like to talk to you about Jude Williams."

"What about him?" she said as she started to hint at a frown. "We're just friends, no matter what anybody else says. He helped me clean out my attic last month, and we struck up a conversation. There's nothing more to it than that."

Grace stepped forward and asked, "Lisa, you haven't heard about what happened to Jude yet, have you?"

"What are you talking about? The police chief didn't arrest him for doing something silly, did he? Did it have something to do with me?" She started to go back inside. "I'll straighten this all out. I'm sure that it's just a harmless misunderstanding."

"Lisa, Jude is dead," I said softly.

"What! He can't be dead!".

"I'm afraid it's true," Grace added. "I'm sorry. We just assumed that you knew."

"How did it happen?" she asked me.

"From what we've heard, he was hit in the back of the head with an iron bar last night."

Lisa didn't want to believe it; that much was clear. I thought it odd that she glanced back inside her house for a second before she spoke again. She was fighting back tears, but she still managed to keep most of her cool. "If you're telling me the truth, then why are you here?"

"We found this in his room when we searched it a few minutes ago," I said as I held the book up.

"Let me see that," she snapped as she tried to grab it out of my hands.

I was ready for her, though, so I pulled it back just in time. "If you don't mind, we're going to hold onto that. What we want to know is what it was doing on Jude's nightstand."

"I loaned it to him," she said uncertainly, as though she wasn't sure that was the final story she was going to stick to. "I want it back now, though. It's mine."

"You'll have to ask Chief Martin for it," I said. "We were on our way to deliver it to him, but we thought we'd stop by here first and give you a chance to explain its presence yourself."

"I already told you. Jude and I were friends. There was nothing more to it than that."

"That doesn't explain the picture on his cellphone we found," Grace said. I turned to look at her in shock. Not only hadn't I found any photos of Lisa or anyone else, I hadn't even *seen* his phone.

I turned back to her to explain when I saw her brave face start to crumble. "He told me that he erased all of those," she said, her voice ragged with tears.

I wanted to assure her that he might have, but Grace stepped forward again. "They were hard to find, so maybe nobody else will see them. How long had you two been having an affair?"

"Just a month, but I broke it off two days ago."

"Is there anyone else who can confirm that?" Grace asked.

"I didn't exactly tell anyone when it started, so why would I tell them when I ended it?" Lisa said. "And keep your voice down, would you? My husband's in the living room taking a nap."

"We'll do our best," I said. "Lisa, did Frank have any idea about what you were up to?" I asked softly.

She looked shocked by the very idea of it. "Are you crazy? If he even suspected, things would have gone horribly wrong for Jude and me both." The realization that something had indeed happened to Jude hit her at that moment. "No. No. I don't believe it. Frank would never do it."

"Never do what?" a sleepy gruff man's voice asked from the house.

Lisa was at a loss for an explanation, but Grace stepped right up. "We thought you ordered three dozen donuts. They're back in Suzanne's Jeep. Should we go on and bring them in?"

I hoped he didn't say yes, since we didn't even have a

donut hole on us at the time.

"I never ordered any donuts," he said roughly. "What are you trying to pull here?"

"Nothing at all," I said. "My mistake." How were we going to get out of this in one piece?

Grace tapped my shoulder, and as I turned toward her, she pulled a small pad from her purse as she said, "Look, these are for an address in Union Square. It was just a mix-up all along."

I pretended to study her grocery list for a moment before I said, "You're right. Sorry to bother you both."

"Hang on a second," Frank said ominously, and I waited for one of his meaty paws to descend on my shoulder.

"Yes?" I asked.

"What kind of donuts are we talking about here?"

This one I could answer myself. "They're special order, so I'm afraid they aren't for sale. Sorry again to trouble you both."

"Whatever," he said as he went back into the house.

"Thank you," Lisa said softly.

"Frank's going to find out sooner or later," I said. "You really should tell us everything you can about who might have wanted to kill Jude."

"Do you mean besides his crazy old aunt, Gabby Williams?"

"Besides her," I said. I doubted that Gabby had done it, but even if she had, I wasn't going to leave it at that. "Who else might have wanted to harm him, Lisa?"

"You really should talk to Reggie Nance. He's been gunning for Jude since I've known him."

That was the second time I'd heard Reggie's name mentioned that day linked to Jude. "You mean about his daughter?" I asked.

"You'd better believe it. That man was crazy. He even threatened to kill Jude right in front of me," she said.

"I already had his name on my list," I said. "Surely there has to be someone else."

Lisa seemed to think about it for a moment. "The only other person I can think of is Peter Hickman."

Hearing her say the name of Max's best man really threw me. He'd been the last name I'd expected to hear from Lisa as a possible suspect. "What does Peter have to do with it?" I asked.

"He's the one who beat Jude up yesterday. He wasn't the only one to score a few punches, though. Peter got messed up himself. You know what? You should really talk to—"

From the other room, we all heard Frank call out, "Lisa? What are you still doing out there?"

"I've got to go," she said breathlessly, but before she left, she hesitated for a moment. "Poor Jude. What a sad waste. How big was the bar that killed him?"

That was an unusual question, one I didn't have the answer to. "I'm not sure, but I doubt that it was light. Why do you ask?"

"No reason," she said quickly, and then Lisa darted back inside, closing the door hard behind her.

"That was interesting," Grace said.

"What made you lie about his cellphone?" I asked her as we walked back to my Jeep. "Saying we had a donut delivery was really clever of you, but talking about pictures that we couldn't have seen was something else entirely."

"I'm sorry, Suzanne. I could tell that she was holding something back, and that she was afraid of something. It seemed like the next logical step to me."

"I don't know about that," I said. "I wouldn't have thought about bluffing like that in a million years."

"I can't tell," Grace said with a slight smile. "Are you congratulating me on using initiative, or are you scolding me for stepping over the line?"

"Why can't it be a little bit of both?" I asked.

"I suppose that it can," Grace said. "You're right, though. I probably shouldn't have said that last bit."

"I just worry that if Lisa is innocent, you've given her some sleepless nights ahead of her. You might have struck gold this time, but I really don't like lying to the people we question, at least not about something as serious as that. Okay?"

"Okay," she said somberly. "I'll watch my step in the future."

"Just don't give anybody nightmares if you can help it," I said with a smile.

"Except the killer, of course," she added.

"You can do whatever you'd like to the murderer. I'll even help if I get the chance."

"Fair enough. Where should we go now?"

I didn't even have to think about it. "I've never been a big fan of Peter Hickman's, but we need to go to Max's to see him next. I suspected that he got into a fight with someone after what Emily told me yesterday, and after what Lisa just said, it was clearly Jude. What I want to know is who started it, who finished it, and what was it all about in the first place?"

"Those are all good questions," Grace said. "Should I ask him myself?"

I was surprised by the offer. "Thanks, but I can handle him just fine."

"I wasn't trying to overstep," Grace said. "I just know that you two have a long history of disliking each other, so if I can make it go smoother, I'm happy to step in."

"Let me lead off, and if I need you, feel free to jump in," I said.

"I'd be delighted."

"Only try not to go so far off script this time, okay?"

"I promise," she said.

I knew that Grace had meant well, and this time she'd actually struck gold with her assumptions, but I didn't like running an investigation that way. We were on the hunt for a killer, and I knew that I couldn't afford to be squeamish about the tactics we used, but I also had to live with most of these folks long after the murder had been solved, and I didn't want to make any enemies that I didn't have to in the process of tracking down the killer. Besides, I wanted to be able to sleep at night myself, and I wasn't sure that I'd be able to do it if I started accusing folks of all kinds of unacceptable behavior without a lick of proof to back any of it up. I might not be as successful operating that way, but if that was the biggest consequence of my actions, I could live with it.

Chapter 9

The only problem was that Peter was nowhere to be found.

To make matters worse, Max was gone as well. Peter *had* to be staying with my ex-husband, so I was disappointed when no one answered the door when we knocked.

I turned to say something to Grace when I spotted a car starting up and driving away from the way that we'd just come. "Who was that?" I asked her.

"I don't know. Should we follow them?"

"Come on. Jump into the Jeep."

We started after the car, and I caught one glimpse of the man driving before he lost me.

It was Reggie Nance.

Why would he be staking out Max's house? Was he after my ex, or Peter? Why would he want to have words with either one of them? After all, the man he'd threatened to kill was already dead. Was Reggie taking care of *all* of his old grudges, and did that mean that he'd started with Jude and was about to move on to the next name on his list?

"We lost him," Grace said.

"That's okay," I said as I stopped and turned around in someone's driveway.

"Why are you taking this so calmly?" she asked me.

"Because I saw who it was," I said as I drove at easier pace.

"Don't keep it a secret from me. Who was it?"

"Reggie Nance," I said.

"What would Reggie want with Max or Peter?"

"I can't figure that, either, but wouldn't you like to ask him for yourself?"

"So, that's where we're going now," Grace said.

"Unless you have any objections," I answered.

"No, ma'am. You're in the driver's seat for this thing, and I mean that literally."

We pulled up in front of Reggie Nance's house, and I was surprised to see that his car was pulled up in front. If I hadn't seen him myself, I might have believed that he'd been there all along.

"Suzanne, how sure are you that it was Reggie that you saw?"

"I'm pretty sure," I said as I parked the Jeep behind his car and got out. I put a hand on his car hood, and it was hot to the touch. "Feel that," I said to Grace.

She did as I asked then pulled her hand quickly away. "Wow, he must have raced straight over here. Let's go see where the fire was."

"Let's take this one easy, okay?" I asked her.

"Okay by me. You lead, and I'll follow." Grace paused, looked around the overgrown lawn and the house with its chipped paint, and then she added, "He's really let this place go downhill, hasn't he?"

"You should have seen it when Debbie was alive. She made it into a showplace for her father, but I guess he just lost the heart to keep it up."

"It's tragic all the way around, isn't it?" Grace asked sadly.

"It is." I knocked on the door, and Reggie answered, toweling off his hair. It was clear that he was trying to make it look as though he'd just gotten out of the shower, but I knew better. There was no way he would have time to do that since we'd seen him racing away in his car.

"What can I do for you, Suzanne?"

"First, you can drop the act," I said.

"What are you talking about?"

"We saw you in front of Max's place three minutes ago. You barely had time to wash your hands, let alone take a shower."

"I don't know what you're talking about. I've been here all afternoon," he said as he finished drying his hair and threw the towel over his shoulder. I would have liked to wrap it around his neck. I *hated* being lied to.

"Then why is the hood of your car hot enough to fry eggs on?" Grace asked.

"The sun must be warmer than it feels," Reggie insisted.

"Are you really going to try to play it that way?" I asked. Grace had just asked the question I'd been about to ask myself, so I couldn't exactly get mad at her for jumping on it.

"Like I said, you lost me. Now, if you'll excuse me, I've got things to do."

He closed the door on us, not quite slamming it in our faces, but it was close enough.

"He's lying to us," Grace said.

"I'm just glad that *you* believe me. If I hadn't felt his car hood, I'd be having doubts myself."

"Suzanne, I trust your word over anyone I know. If you say it was Reggie at Max's place, then it was Reggie. Besides, that hood was hot!"

"Thanks for believing me," I said. I decided that there was nothing that we could do now, so I turned and started back to my Jeep.

"Are we just going to give up and go away?" Grace asked as she stood firmly on the porch.

"No, but this angle of attack clearly didn't work. We're going to have to be a little craftier if we're going to learn anything from Reggie Nance."

"Ooh, I love crafty," she said. "Just as long as you mean sneaky by it."

"That's what I mean. I'm just not sure I know how to go about it."

"Don't worry," Grace said. "I'm sure that your devious mind will come up with something."

"Thanks, I think," I said as we got in and I started the

engine.

"Oh, it was a compliment," Grace said. "We still have a little bit of time before dinner. Do you have any other ideas about where we can go now?"

I was about to answer when my cellphone rang. "Hang on one second," I said as I turned the engine back off. Was Jake finally getting back to me?

It was Emily instead. "Hi, Emily," I said. "What's going on?"

"Suzanne, did I catch you at a bad time?" she asked.

I had to cheer up, and fast. My friend was getting married, and she was counting on me. "No, not at all. How are things going?"

"Mother has things moving like clockwork. It's as though she's spent her entire life planning for this wedding, and there's no stopping her. I'm beginning to wonder who's more excited about this wedding, her or me."

"She's just happy for you," I said. "Would you like me to say something to her?"

"Oh, no, I wouldn't ask you to do that. She'll be fine."

"Then what can I do to make your life easier?"

"You can tell me your plans for the wedding donuts," she said. "It's just about the only thing on the list that Mom is letting someone else handle, and she keeps asking me what you've got in mind."

Honestly, I hadn't had much time to think about it, let alone come up with any ideas I thought might work. I couldn't exactly tell her that, though. "I'm kicking around a few overall concepts at the moment. I know that you like your donuts loaded with toppings, and Max will eat anything, but do you have any special requests for your guests?" Maybe she'd give me something to go on.

"No, I trust your judgment," she said. "Can you at least give me a hint about what you're considering?"

"I don't want to spoil any surprises for you until I get

all of the details worked out," I said.

"I understand that," she said, though she sounded a little disappointed. "I know there's not much time, Suzanne, but if anybody can do it, you can."

"I appreciate the show of faith in me," I said.

"Emma told me that you were a genius with donuts, so who am I to contradict her?" Emily asked with a laugh, and then she hung up.

"Remind me to thank my assistant for raising the bride's expectations beyond belief," I muttered to myself.

I must have said it louder than I'd planned, because Grace asked, "What did Emma say?"

"That wasn't Emma; it was Emily," I said. "Evidently the bride is expecting a donut extravaganza for her wedding reception."

"It's kind of a quirky idea, isn't it?" Grace asked me.

"Quirky is the nicest thing you can say about it," I replied. "Change of plans. I need to start planning this donut display, and I mean right now."

"Would you like some help? I'm not sure how much actual aid I can deliver, but I'm great at providing moral support."

"I'll take what I can get," I said. "Let me call Momma and see what's for dinner."

"You know me. I'll eat *anything* your mother makes," Grace answered with a smile.

"I would to, but I have to make sure that she's going to be there."

I called Momma's number, and she picked up on the fourth ring. "Suzanne, are you coming home soon? Dinner is nearly ready."

"That sounds great. Is there room enough for one more?"

"Is Jake coming?" she asked hopefully.

"No, it's just Grace," I said as I glanced over at my best friend.

Grace looked more amused by the comment than anything else, and I mouthed, "Sorry" to her. She just shrugged, but she was smiling all the same.

"Grace would be lovely," Momma said. "Don't worry about a thing. I've got plenty of food."

"See you soon, then."

"I'll be here," Momma said.

After I hung up, Grace asked, "*Just* Grace?"

"She thought that Jake might be coming," I explained.

My friend's smile softened. "I wonder why you haven't heard from him yet?"

"No doubt he's extremely busy," I answered quickly. This was definitely not a subject I wanted to discuss, with Grace or anyone else. "By the way, you're welcome to join us for dinner," I said.

"I appreciate that. Should we start planning the wedding donuts now, or should we wait until we've got full stomachs?"

"I don't think that there's a second to lose," I said as I headed back home. "I'll get Momma's advice, too, but we need to start brainstorming about this right now on the drive home."

Unfortunately, we weren't able to come up with anything that didn't sound ridiculous by the time we pulled into the drive at the cottage. I parked my Jeep, and Grace and I walked up the steps together. Jake was constantly on my mind, but I knew that it would be foolish to try to get in touch with him now. Most likely he was too busy to talk to me.

At least that's what I hoped was the reason that he hadn't gotten back in touch with me yet.

The second I walked through the door, the aromas of barbequed chicken hit me full on. "Momma, you've outdone yourself."

"I hope you like it," she said. "The chicken was on sale at the supermarket, so I added some veggies, too. I know how much you love sizzling yams, tiny potatoes, and baby carrots."

"Thanks for including me," Grace said as she hugged my mother and kissed her cheek.

"Goodness, you should know that you are always welcome here. Wash up, ladies, and I'll get a few last-minute things settled here."

Grace went to wash her hands, and I called out to her, "I'll be right there."

I hugged my mother, and as I did, I whispered in her ear, "Thank you."

"Of course," she said as she hugged me tightly. "Why exactly are you thanking me, Suzanne? Not that I'm not appreciative."

"For being here, and always taking my side, no matter what," I said with a grin as I pulled away.

"Goodness, I can't imagine being any other way," she said as she returned my grin.

We'd had our share of issues over the years, but I loved where we were right now in our relationship. "Now, I'd better wash up, too."

"Don't worry; we'll wait for you. Perhaps," she added with a twinkle in her eye. Momma was definitely happier these days, and I knew that Chief Martin being in her life had a great deal to do with it. That factor alone had made me more willing to accept the man for what he was, and in turn, he'd begun to trust my unofficial capabilities more. I knew that something *might* derail our new spirit of cooperation, though, so I planned to enjoy it all while I could.

I took a chicken leg, basted in sauce and simmering in the oven for an hour, and helped myself to some of the veggies my mother was so good at making. After cutting them into chunks, she drizzled them in olive oil and added a little sea salt, then roasted them in the oven. They were incredible, each bite perfectly done, crisp on the outside and perfect inside. The chicken was moist and juicy, and I added a little of Momma's sauce from the pan to top mine off.

After we'd eaten, Momma said, "It always amazes me how good something can be that doesn't cost all that much to prepare and serve."

"You don't give yourself enough credit," Grace said. "I could take the exact same ingredients and render them into something entirely inedible."

"I'm sure you're just being too hard on yourself."

"Obviously you've never tasted her cooking," I said with a smile.

Grace laughed at my comment. "You're one to talk."

"Hey, I'm a specialist more than a general chef. I might not be able to do much besides make donuts, but I'm *very* good at what I do."

"Agreed," Grace said as she stood and started gathering dishes.

Momma stood as well. "Grace, leave those to me."

"We don't mind helping," I said as I joined them as they cleared the table. "After all, it's the least that we can do."

Normally Momma might fight me on it, but this time she just smiled. "If you're sure you two don't mind, I've gotten into a new mystery that I just can't put down. It's about a diner, of all things, if you can imagine that."

"Is it all about the food?" Grace asked. "I might like to read that myself when you're finished."

"Not just comfort food, but crime solving, too," Momma said. "There's a large family working at the diner itself, but the main amateur detectives are a granddaughter and her grandfather. I'll be honest with you. I hesitated to start reading books electronically at first, but once I took the plunge, I was sold."

"Sometimes they make life easier than toting books around, don't they?" I said. "My book group has been picking some huge books lately, and I have to admit, I enjoy the rest it gives my arms not having to hold a paper book up at night."

"Go on and read," Grace said. "We've got this."

As we cleared the dishes and put the leftovers away in the fridge, Grace asked me, "Have you come up with any new ideas?"

"About who killed Jude?" I asked.

"No, I was wondering what you were going to do about the wedding donuts."

I hit my forehead. "Honestly, I forgot all about them."

"Well, you'd better come up with *something*," Grace said. "Emily's expecting miracles from you, and if I know her mother, she's not going to accept anything less than perfection."

"After we finish the dishes, let's invite Momma to brainstorm with us. She'll get a kick out of it, and I could use all of the help I can get."

"I'm all for it," Grace said.

We made short work of the dishes, and when we came into the living room, we found Momma engrossed in her e-reader.

"Do you have a minute?" I asked her.

"Of course," she said as she turned it off and put it on the coffee table. "What can I do for you?"

"I'm afraid that I might be in over my head with something," I said.

Momma just smiled. "It wouldn't be the first time that I've ever heard that in your life."

I laughed, recalling the times in the past that I'd said the exact same thing. "It's different this time, since Emily wants me to create wedding donuts for the reception in honor of the role I played in getting her and Max together."

"Personally, I think it's a wonderful idea."

"You don't think it's a little unconventional?" I asked her.

"Suzanne, being the maid of honor in your ex-husband's wedding sort of threw conventionality out the window, wouldn't you say?"

"So, what are your thoughts?" I asked.

"How about devil's food cake donuts for the groom, and angel-food cake donuts for the bride?" she asked with that grin of hers.

"That's it," I said. "It's perfect."

"Suzanne, I was just joking," Momma said.

"You may have been," Grace replied for me, "but I think it's excellent, too. Suzanne, you can ice the angel food cake donuts with white icing, and the devil's-food cake with chocolate. Done and done."

"Hang on. Before we get too excited about this, I need to run it by Emily first," I said as I reached for my cellphone. "She might not find it as amusing as we do."

A few minutes later, I hung up and stared at Grace and Momma.

"What did she say?" Grace asked.

"She loved it," I said. "Momma, you hit a home run with that idea."

"I hope you didn't tell her that it came from me, Suzanne," Momma said.

"I told her that it was a group effort after much consultation and deliberation," I replied with a grin. "Why, did you want solo credit?"

"No, I can live with what you said just fine." I saw her looking at her e-reader. "Was there anything else I could do to help?"

"No, you can go back to your book," I said as I kissed her cheek. "Thanks again. You're a genius."

"Hardly," Momma said, but she wasn't entirely unhappy about my praise.

"Now that that particular dilemma is solved, I'd better take off," Grace said.

"It's early still, and that's coming from a woman who has to get up in the middle of the night," I replied.

"I know, but if we're going to go sleuthing tomorrow

afternoon, I have some work to do at home tonight. I'll
see you tomorrow at eleven," she said.

"Let me at least walk you out," I said.

"Sounds great. Good night," Grace said to my mother
as she left.

"Night, dear. Pleasant dreams."

After Grace was gone, I came back in and told
Momma, "I think I'll try to catch up on some of that
sleep I've been missing lately."

"We both know that you can *never* catch up," Momma
said.

"No, but I can make a stab at it. I'll see you
tomorrow."

I don't even think she heard me. That must be some
book. After she finished it, I was going to see if I could
borrow it myself.

It sounded like a real winner.

I tried not to think about Jake as I lay in bed, but it was
hard not to. What was going on with that man? I
couldn't imagine him not being in my life. If he'd just
tell me what was wrong, I might be able to fix it, but this
silence was just driving me crazy. I'd have to find a
way to track him down tomorrow even if I had to drive
to Raleigh to do it.

I wasn't going to give up without giving it everything I
had.

After I came to that conclusion, sleep came much
easier than I'd expected, but my alarm clock still rang
much too early for my taste.

Chapter 10

It had been business as usual at the donut shop the next day when I was surprised to see Reggie Nance come in. Sure, he'd been a longtime customer of mine, but after the way he'd lied to us the day before, I was kind of shocked to see him show his face at Donut Hearts.

"What can I get you?" I asked him as formally as I could. I wasn't fond of the way he'd acted the day before, but that didn't mean that I could afford to alienate any of my customers at the shop.

"I'll have the usual, Suzanne," he said with a frown.

"Coming right up," I replied as I started selecting a dozen random donuts for his office. It was a weekly ritual of his, and under other circumstances, I would have welcomed his business. After I boxed a good selection, I taped the lid and slid the box across the counter. I quoted the price, and Reggie paid promptly.

He started to pick the donuts up when he hesitated. "Those smell really good today. I think I have time for a coffee and a glazed donut here."

In all the time he'd been coming to Donut Hearts, he'd never lingered at the shop. What was going on?

"Absolutely," I said as I quoted him an additional price.

He paid, and I put his coffee and donut on a tray. "There you go."

"I'll just eat this at the counter, if that's all right with you."

I nodded. "It's fine."

I turned my back and started consolidating donuts on the trays so Emma could start washing the empty ones when Reggie cleared his voice and spoke up. "Do you have a second?"

"I've got all the time in the world. I can work and talk at the same time," I said, keeping my back to him.

Reggie wasn't going to allow that, though. "Suzanne,

look at me. I want to talk to you."

I put the tray down and turned to face him. "Go on. You've got my undivided attention."

"I'm sorry I lied to you yesterday," he said as his words came out in a rush. It was pretty clear that he wasn't all that used to apologizing to *anyone*, and it was difficult for him to do.

"I am, too," I said. "I thought we were friends."

"I'd like to think that myself," Reggie replied.

"In my book, friends don't lie to each other," I said with a frown.

"I panicked, okay? I didn't want anyone to know that I was watching Max's place." His voice was so low it was hard to hear him, and I was standing pretty close by. There were a few folks in the donut shop, but I doubted that anyone else could hear us.

"What were you doing there, anyway?" I asked as I took a step closer.

"I wanted to ask Max's friend, Peter, if he was the one who killed Jude," Reggie said.

"What! Why would you ask him that?"

"I saw them fighting, Suzanne. It's not that far a leap to go from a fistfight to murder."

"Excuse me for saying so, but I know that you didn't have any affection for Jude yourself. Why would you care if Peter killed him?"

"You're probably not going to understand this, but I was going to give him a reward," Reggie said.

"A reward? Like a bounty? Are you kidding me?" What had happened to the friendly guy I'd known all these years?

"Jude Williams killed my daughter just as surely as if he'd put a gun to her head and pulled the trigger," Reggie said. "Maybe I didn't have the guts to do anything about Jude myself, but I wanted to shake the hand of the guy who did, and show him my appreciation."

"Reggie, that's just plain wrong. What would Debbie think if she knew what you were doing?" I asked it without thinking, but it was a fair question. I'd known Debbie Nance, and one thing I was pretty sure of was that she wouldn't approve of her father's current vengeful attitude.

"Leave her out of this, Suzanne," Reggie said with a hard edge in his voice.

"How can I? She's at the center of this whole thing for you."

"You don't have kids. You can't know what it's like to lose one," Reggie said. His stern face began to crack, and tears ran unnoticed down his cheeks.

"I may not have children, but I know what it's like to lose someone you love," I said, thinking of my late father.

"Losing a child is different. Why did I even try to come here to explain myself to you? You'll *never* be able to understand what I've been through."

Reggie started for the door, leaving his donuts behind. "Hey, don't forget these," I called out.

"Keep them," he said as he hurried away. "I don't want them anymore."

I shook my head, wondering why I'd talked to him the way I had. Reggie was right about one thing. I had no idea what it was like to lose a child. That didn't justify his behavior, but it did help to explain it. If he'd been telling me the truth about not killing Jude, it would take his name off of my list of suspects, but I wasn't ready to take him off at his word just yet.

I needed to do more digging before I was ready to do that.

Still, his visit certainly gave me something to think about.

"Aren't you closed yet?" Grace asked as she walked into Donut Hearts a few minutes before eleven.

"Just be glad that I'm not still open until noon," I said as I finished boxing up the donuts we had left over from the morning's sales. I loved it when we had around a dozen unsold donuts at the end of the workday, but I absolutely hated it when we had to shut down early because we were out of inventory. Most days I usually erred on the side of caution and made too many donuts. After all, I could always give them away to the church, or even use the extras to help pave the way as I questioned suspects.

"I don't know how you keep open *this* late in the morning, considering the time you get started," she said. "I've just been up two hours and I'm already ready for a nap."

"I'm willing to bet that you were up later than I was last night, though," I replied. I crammed the thirteenth donut into the box and set it on the countertop. As I pulled the trays and handed them to Emma, I asked, "Did you call in sick today?"

"I didn't have to. Officially, I'm working on employee evaluations." Grace grinned at me as she added, "I did them last night, though, so you've got me all day today."

"Does your boss have any idea how you work their system?" I asked with a smile.

"She doesn't want to, Suzanne. I'm running the number three territory in the Southeast. As long as the numbers are good, no one asks me any questions."

"It must be nice," I said as I wiped the counter down.

"It has its moments," she said. Grace looked back into the kitchen where Emma was happily washing the last dishes, glasses, cups, and trays for the day. It was clear that my assistant was listening to her iPod by the soft sounds of her singing along with the music. Sometimes I tried to guess based on what I heard, but it was often too hard to do. Emma wasn't exactly tone deaf, but she wasn't spot-on in her sing-alongs, either. "What's on the schedule for this afternoon?"

"Do you mean after I finish cleaning up here, closing out the register, making my deposit out, and generally shutting the donut shop down for the day?"

"Yeah, after all of that," Grace said with a grin. "Don't try to complain to me about what you do. You know as well as I do that you love it."

"Guilty as charged," I said as I returned her smile. "We need to find Peter and talk to him. That's got to be first on our list."

"Do you really think that he might have killed Jude?" Grace asked.

"I don't know, but there's enough smoke around that I'm willing to look for some fire."

"Okay, so we talk to Peter. What's in store after that?" Grace said as she flipped open the box of donuts. She was trying to eat healthier these days, but that didn't mean that she was willing to cut donuts completely out of her life.

"You can have one, you know," I said.

"What? No. No thanks. No offense," she said as she closed the lid and scooted the donuts back toward me. "I've picked up a few pounds lately that I've been trying to lose."

"You look great, and you know it," I said as I moved them out of her reach.

"Yes, we're all pretty," she said happily. "Are we going to talk to Max, too?"

"We have to, don't we?" I asked.

"Well, Jude used to go out with Emily, and Max is the jealous type, so yes, he needs to be on our list."

"That's going to be more awkward than I can even fathom," I said.

"I could do it by myself, if you'd like me to," Grace offered.

"Thanks, but I'll manage to get through it," I replied. "Should we talk to Emily as well?"

"Do you honestly think that *she* might have killed Jude?" Grace asked, the surprise clear on her face.

"I don't know, but we have to ask," I said.

"What motive could she possibly have?"

"What if Jude threatened to tell Max something that would break up the wedding?" I asked. "She might kill him to protect her love."

"What could he say that could possibly drive Max away?" Grace asked. "The man's absolutely smitten with her. You said as much yourself."

"That's just it. I don't know. We need to find *anyone* Jude interacted with in the last few days who might have a reason to want to see him dead."

"That could be a long list of suspects," Grace said after whistling softly.

"Then we'd better get started."

"Is there anything else we need to do today?"

There was something else on my personal list, but I wasn't about to tell Grace that I was going to track Jake down, even if I had to drive to Raleigh to do it. I was going to find out what my boyfriend had on his mind, one way or the other. If he was going to dump me, I needed to get it over with. I honestly was beginning to think that the suspense of it all was worse than anything that he could say to me. That wasn't exactly true, but I did hate being kept in the dark about his intentions. "Nothing I can't handle on my own."

"Are you talking about Jake?" she asked tentatively.

"I really don't want to discuss it," I said.

She could read my tone of voice better than anybody but my mother could. Grace recognized the fact that I was ending the conversation before it could even get started. "Okay, what can I do to help around here so we can get started?" she asked as she clapped her hands together and looked around the donut shop.

"You could wipe the tables down and sweep the floor," I said.

"Consider it done," she said. Grace grabbed a rag, and I started balancing the register receipts and running my daily reports. Everything checked out on the first try, and I was just finishing up the deposit slip when Emma walked out.

"The dishes are done, and the kitchen floor is clean. Is there anything else I can do?"

"Would you mind running this by the bank on your way home?" I asked her as I held the bag holding our deposit up in the air.

"Happy to do it," she said. "I'll see you in the morning."

"I'll be here," I said as I let her out the locked door.

Grace and Emma exchanged good-byes of their own. Once Emma was gone, I turned to my best friend, and as I grabbed our leftover donuts to take with us, I said, "Let's get started. Thanks for helping me close the shop."

"Glad to do it. So, is it back to Max's first?"

"It's as good a place to start as any," I said. "I just hope they're both there."

"Given that it's not even noon yet, I'm willing to bet that they're both still asleep."

"You might be right. If they are, what do you say we go wake them up?"

"Lead the way. I'm right behind you," Grace said as we walked out of the shop and locked the door behind us. Any more donutmaking would have to wait until tomorrow.

For now, it was time for us to dig into the reason someone had murdered Jude Williams.

Chapter 11

"Hey, Suzanne," Peter Hickman said as he opened the door to Max's place when I knocked. "If you're looking for your ex-hubby, he's in the shower." Peter was wearing a bathrobe, and I held my breath hoping that it stayed together. It was obvious that he had just woken up, given his disheveled hair and his bloodshot eyes.

"That's quite a black eye you've got there," I said.

"This? It's nothing. You should see the other guy," Peter said.

"Is that supposed to be funny?" Grace asked with a whip in her voice.

Peter looked at her warily. "What put the burr under your saddle, Grace?" he asked her.

"Are you trying to claim that you don't know that Jude Williams is dead?" I asked him point-blank.

Peter pursed his lips. "*Now* who's saying things in bad taste?"

"It's true, Peter. Are you telling me that you didn't already know?" I asked.

"How am I supposed to know if you're even telling me the truth?" Peter asked. After studying our faces, he must have finally realized that we wouldn't joke about something like that. "It's really true, isn't it? How did it happen?"

Grace was about to answer when I shook my head slightly. She stopped, and I asked, "Why don't you let me ask the questions? Why were you two fighting so publicly?"

Peter's hand went automatically to his bruised eye. "What makes you think we were fighting?"

"Come on; we're not stupid, Peter. We know what happened." There was no way that he was going to bluff his way out of this one. We had reliable witnesses on our side.

"You just *think* you know," Peter said. A little reluctantly, he added, "I guess you might as well come on inside. Max needs to hear this, too."

"Why is that?" I asked him as Grace and I followed him inside.

"Because apparently he's in this just as deeply as I am," Peter said.

I felt my blood run cold hearing that.

It appeared that my ex was in some serious trouble, and right before he was set to marry one of my dearest friends. The fact that I'd played such a significant role in the matchmaking didn't help matters one little bit, either.

Max walked out of the shower with a towel around his waist. He was using another one to dry his hair, and when he saw us, he grinned. "What brings you two here so bright and early?"

"Max, somebody killed Jude Williams," Peter said before either one of us could respond.

"You got a few shots in, but you have to give the man credit. He did just as much damage to you," Max said with that ever-present grin of his. "If anything, I'd call it a draw. Nobody won, nobody lost, and nobody certainly got killed."

"Jude is in the morgue right now, Max," I said. "He's dead."

"But I don't understand," my ex said. "Peter didn't hit him that hard."

"Actually, I've been trying to deny the fact that I even got into a fight with him in the first place," Peter said. "You kind of just ruined it for me there, buddy."

"Peter, I wasn't the only one who saw what happened. You didn't do anything wrong. Jude picked that fight, and we both know it."

"Where have you two been?" I asked. "This all just happened."

Max looked at me sheepishly as he explained, "Peter's

bachelor party idea went a little longer than we expected it to."

"*That's* what you've been doing all this time?" I asked incredulously.

Max smiled at me before he said, "Suzanne, as much as I appreciate your concern, you don't have the right to use that tone of voice with me anymore. I explained it all to Emily before we left, and she was perfectly fine with it."

"Or she just said that she was," Grace said, skepticism thick in her voice.

"She understands me," Max said. "That's why we're getting married."

"Well, I've got a hunch nobody's doing anything until Chief Martin talks to you both. I'm surprised he hasn't been here yet."

"He might have left a few messages," Max admitted reluctantly.

"And you weren't even a *little* curious about what he wanted?" Grace asked him.

"I thought he was sending along his best wishes," Max said.

The front doorbell rang, and Max answered it without thinking.

It was the police chief, and he clearly wasn't happy with any of us. "What are you two doing here?" he asked Grace and me the second he saw us standing together.

"We just wanted to have a little chat with Max and Peter," I said.

"Get in line," he said as he turned to my ex and his best friend. "Gentlemen, get dressed."

"We just heard the news about Jude Williams, and that's the truth," Max said.

"Save it. I don't want to get into it right here. Unless you object, and you'd better have a darn good reason if you do, this interview is going to take place in my office. Do either one of you have any problem with that?" The way he stared at them both, it was clear that the question was moot. He nodded at their lack of responses. "Good. Now go."

Once they were back in Max's bedroom, Chief Martin turned to us. "Really? You just couldn't wait, could you?"

"We've been trying to track them down ourselves," I said.

"What did they say?"

"They both claimed they didn't know that Jude was dead," I said.

"Do you believe them?"

"Yes," Grace said quickly.

When I didn't answer right away, the chief asked, "Well? What about you, Suzanne?"

"I'd *like* to be able to say that I do, but they *are* both decent actors. Maybe they were telling the truth, or maybe they're just both very good at lying. I don't know, and that's the truth."

"I appreciate your candor," the chief said.

Both men came out in jeans and T-shirts. "We'll follow you out," I said.

"Do me a favor, would you?" Max asked me as we all walked out together.

"Sure," I said.

"Don't tell Emily about this."

"Max, I'm not comfortable keeping secrets from her," I said.

"I'm going to tell her. I just want to do it myself. Can you at least give me that?"

I thought about it, and then I answered, "I won't go out of my way to tell her where you two are, but if she asks me, I'm going to tell her. I'm sorry, but that's the best I can do."

"I'll take it then," he said. "Thanks, Suzanne."

"Happy to help."

"Chief, do you mind if we follow you there in my car?" Max asked.

I could see Chief Martin consider it, and then finally, he nodded. "Stay in my rearview mirror the entire time. If you try to make any unscheduled stops, you won't be happy with the results."

"You've got it," Max said.

Peter waved to us as he got into Max's car, but he looked a little concerned as he did so. Then again, who could blame him? He'd had a fistfight with a man who was murdered soon afterward. It couldn't feel good, no matter how you looked at it.

Once everyone was gone, Grace turned to me. "There goes two of our suspects," she said. "Does this change our plans in any way?"

"I'm thinking that it might be a good time to see if we can get Lisa Grambling alone. I had a hunch that the last time we spoke, she had more to say."

"Oh, boy. This should be a real treat," Grace said as we both got into my Jeep and drove over to Lisa's place.

I just hoped that Frank would be gone this time.

Otherwise, I had a hunch that we weren't going to get a thing out of her.

"I don't want to talk to either one of you," Lisa Grambling said as she opened her front door.

"Why, is your husband still at home?" I whispered. "We can meet up someplace else if you'd like." I had to get this woman alone so she could speak frankly about Jude Williams.

"He's at work," Lisa said. "That still doesn't change the way I feel. You both need to stop bothering me, or I'll tell Frank that you're harassing me."

"You were eager enough to talk to us yesterday," Grace said. "What's changed?"

"We're finished here," Lisa said. Before she ducked back inside though, she looked quickly up and down the

street. The look in her eyes could only be described as real fear.

"Lisa, has someone threatened you? If your husband is being abusive, you need to get out."

"My husband loves me," she said emphatically.

"Then who are you so afraid of?" I asked her.

She replied by slamming the door in my face.

"What was that all about?" Grace asked me as we walked back to my Jeep and got in.

"She's clearly rattled about something. Do you think it's possible that the killer got to her and threatened her to keep her mouth shut?"

"I can't for the life of me figure out why else she'd have such an abrupt change in attitude. Yesterday she couldn't stop herself from naming suspects in Jude's murder, and today she acted as though she was afraid of something, or someone. How else can we read it?"

I nodded. "I know you're right, but what good will it do us knowing that Lisa's scared? We don't have any idea who might know that she'd been talking to us."

"Unless someone has been following us," Grace said.

"You're talking about Reggie Nance, aren't you?"

"We have only his word that he was at Max's place waiting for Max and Peter to show up. What if we got it all wrong and he'd been following us all along?"

I considered the possibility. "Wasn't he already at Max's when we got there, though?"

"Did you see his car when we first drove up?" Grace asked me.

I thought about it, and then I said, "I can't be sure. I didn't notice him until he started his car and took off."

"So, he could have pulled in behind us and shut off his engine without us noticing him. We were pretty focused on Max's place at the time."

"It's possible," I said.

"Then we need to have a chat with Reggie," Grace said.

"I already spoke with him today. He stormed off without his donuts."

Grace nodded. "Then it's a good thing you had extras this morning."

"What do you expect me to do with those?" I asked her, even though I had a sneaking suspicion what her plan was for my leftovers.

"Why, you're going to apologize, of course, and offer these as a peace offering," she said with a smile.

I wanted to argue the strategy with her, but I knew that she was right. "That's exactly what I'm going to do, and you're going to be standing right beside me when he do."

"There's nowhere else that I'd rather be," Grace said.

"Just one thing," I said as I started the Jeep and drove toward Reggie's office. "It's a minor point, but it's still something that we should probably clear up before we get to his business."

"What's that?"

"What exactly am I apologizing for?" I asked.

"I was hoping that you would be able to come up with something," Grace said with a grin.

"I could say that I was being insensitive about Debbie, but I don't believe that. She wouldn't have approved of her father's attitude. There's no doubt in my mind about that."

"Can you try to fake it?" Grace asked me. "If you can't, I understand, but we need a reason to just show up at his office."

"I *am* sorry if I hurt him," I said. "I don't have to pretend that I'm not."

"There you go, then."

We drove up to the form-supply business Reggie owned and parked in a visitor's parking space. I grabbed the stuffed box of donuts, and then I turned to Grace. "You can sit this one out, if you'd like."

"Are you kidding? This was my idea, remember? Lead on."

"What are we going to say is your reason for being with me?" I asked as we walked up to the front door.

"We have plans this afternoon, so I'm just tagging along when you do this," she said.

"Okay. Here goes."

We walked in through the front door of the business. Three men and women sat at desks behind a counter, though there was room for half a dozen more. They were all on the phone and talking at the same time. I didn't know how I'd be able to get any work done in that kind of environment, but then again, a lot of folks would have balked at the prospect of getting up in the middle of the night to mix batter and dough. To each their own.

There was an unremarkable rather heavyset woman behind the desk that said Reception, so we approached her.

"May I help you?" she asked, her gaze never leaving the box of donuts in my hands.

"We're here to see Reggie," I said.

"Is Mr. Nance expecting you?" she asked.

"No, we don't have an appointment, but this is important. My name's Suzanne Hart, and this is Grace Gauge."

"I know who you are," she said as she looked up briefly from the donuts into my eyes.

"Please. It's important," I said.

"Let me see if Mr. Nance has time to see you."

She left her desk, and Grace whispered to me, "Did you see the way she was eying those donuts?"

"Hey, who can blame her? They're delicious, and she didn't get any today. Reggie left without them, remember?"

"I've got a hunch they aren't leaving with us, no matter what Reggie says."

"Shh. She's coming back."

The woman came back with a frown plastered on her face. "I'm sorry, but Mr. Nance is unavailable. If you'd like me to give him something, I'd be glad to hand deliver it myself."

"Sorry. This has to be done in person, or not at all," Grace piped up.

The woman frowned again, and I could swear I saw storm clouds forming in her eyes. "That's too bad."

I couldn't take it anymore. There was nothing to gain by holding my own donuts hostage. "Why don't you take these anyway?" I asked her as I handed her the box.

"That's really sweet of you," she said with a broad smile. She took the offering and then leaned forward as she whispered, "In ten minutes, he'll be heading to his car to get his hair cut. You can try again outside. I'm sorry, but it's the best that I can do."

"It's perfect," I whispered back. "Thank you."

She just nodded, and Grace and I left the office, but instead of going back to my Jeep, we walked over to Reggie's car. It was parked front and center, and the sign said, "CEO Parking Only." For such a small office, calling yourself a CEO had to show that the man had a bit of an ego.

"Well, what do you know? Your donuts really do open doors, don't they?"

"I wasn't expecting her to be so cooperative. I just hate to disappoint people when they only want my treats, you know?"

"Suzanne, your good heart pays off yet again," Grace said with a smile. "What are we going to say to Reggie now that we've given up our secret weapon?"

"I'm still going to apologize," I said firmly.

"But you don't believe that you need to," Grace protested. "I didn't mean to back you into doing something that you're not comfortable with."

"Grace, he was right. The man lost a daughter in a pretty devastating way right after losing his wife. He has to have felt pain that I can only imagine. I *need* to apologize."

"I knew there was a reason that you were my best friend," Grace said with a soft smile as she hugged me.

"I thought it was because of all the free donuts," I said, trying to soften the seriousness of our conversation.

"Hey, I didn't say that was the *only* reason," she said, joining in with a smile of her own.

It was gone soon enough, though, as Reggie walked outside.

"I told Betty that I wasn't interested in seeing you," Reggie snapped as he barely hesitated upon spying us waiting by his car. "You've got some nerve ambushing me in the parking lot like this."

"I'm sorry," I said, plainly and simply.

It was enough to make Reggie stop. "About what, ambushing me?"

"About what I said about your daughter. I was wrong, and I'm sorry."

That clearly confused him. Reggie had made up his mind to be rough on me, but I'd invoked his daughter's name, and something changed instantly in the man. "That's okay."

"I mean it," I said. "Debbie's memory deserves better than what I gave."

"That it does," he said.

"I can even understand why you'd want to see vengeance for your loss," Grace said.

"Vengeance?" Reggie asked incredulously. "Is that what you two think I'm doing? Justice is more like it. Besides, I didn't touch Jude Williams, as much as I wanted to, and I surely didn't pick up a pipe and hit him with it."

"It was an iron bar," I said. "Reggie, do you happen to have an alibi for the time of the murder?" I asked. "It would make life a great deal easier if you did."

"Who is there to alibi me in the middle of the night?

My family is all gone. I was doing exactly what I do every night, and I was doing it alone. I heated up a frozen dinner, watched a little baseball, and then I fell asleep on the couch. There's no one in the world who saw me, or even spoke to me. But I'm telling you now, once and for all, that I didn't kill Jude Williams. Now, if you'll excuse me, I'm going to be late for my haircut."

Reggie got in and drove away before we could say another word.

"Do you believe him?" Grace asked me after he was gone.

"I want to, but I'm still not sure. How about you?"

Grace shrugged. "You know me. I don't trust anyone. If I see lips moving, I believe that someone is lying to me. Call it the cost of doing business as a saleswoman for too many years. What does your gut tell you?"

"It's surprisingly quiet at the moment," I said, "except rumbling for food. I'm starving, are you?"

"I could eat," she said with a smile. "I'd just about decided to have a few donuts when you gave them away. That should entitle me to a real meal."

"How does the Boxcar Grill sound?" I asked as we got into my Jeep.

"Like a little bit of heaven," she said with a grin.

"Then let's go eat," I replied. We'd managed to get some new information since we'd started our investigation, but we were still nowhere near finding the killer. I was beginning to wonder if we ever would, but I knew that I had to be patient. These things often took time. The problem was that Emily and Max shouldn't have to get married with a cloud of murder hanging over the festivities.

That gave me an artificial time limit, and it was quickly running out.

Chapter 12

"Hey, ladies," Trish said as Grace and I walked into the Boxcar Grill. It was my second favorite place to eat in all of North Carolina, being second only to Napoli's in Union Square. "What's going on with you two today?"

"We've been keeping busy," I said. "What's happening in your world?"

"Just another day in paradise," she said with a grin. "Grab any table you'd like, and I'll be right over. Two sweet teas to start?" she asked.

"Why ruin a long tradition," I said with a grin. "Does that sound good to you, Grace?"

"You know me. I'm easy to please."

Trish and I both started laughing at that clearly false statement, and Grace joined us.

We had just settled into a booth when I noticed someone approaching, obviously intent on speaking with us. I had a hunch that I wasn't going to like it, but I wasn't about to turn tail and run.

"Suzanne, we need to talk," Gabby Williams said as she reached our table.

"Sure thing. Why don't you sit down and join us?" I asked.

Gabby looked around the dining room of the Boxcar. "I don't think so. I don't want the whole town hearing what I've got to say."

"Then let's *all* go outside," Grace said as she started to stand.

"Not you," Gabby said as she looked at my best friend. "Just you," she added as she turned to me.

"Gabby," I said, trying to keep my voice reasonable, "you know that I'm going to tell Grace anything that you tell me as soon as you're gone, don't you?"

"What you do *after* I talk to you is entirely up to you,"

Gabby said, and then she started to walk out of the diner before pausing and asking me, "Aren't you coming?"

"Go on," Grace said. "I don't mind."

"Order for me, would you?" I asked.

"That's dangerous, don't you think?" she asked me with a grin.

"Just know that whatever I get, I might switch with you, so use your best judgment."

"Got it," she said.

"Let's go, Suzanne," Gabby said loudly enough to make every diner turn toward her. "You all need to go back to your food," she told them, and then she stormed out.

I followed along, curious about what she was about to tell me.

Trish asked me softly as I walked past her, "Is everything okay?"

"Not by a long shot, but I'm fine, if that's what you're asking me."

"That's what I wanted to know," she said. "Good luck," Trish added as she gestured toward Gabby.

"Thanks," I said as I walked outside.

Gabby was waiting impatiently for me at a table near the front door down the steps.

"What's so urgent, Gabby?" I asked her.

"I was cleaning up at the house last night and I found something that everyone missed, including you and the cops."

"Was it something in Jude's room?"

"No, this was downstairs stuck in a magazine near his favorite chair."

I hadn't searched the entire house, so I don't know how I could have been expected to find whatever she'd uncovered, but I decided to just let it ride. There was no point getting into an argument with her when she was about to help my investigation. "What did you find?"

"This," she said as she handed me a note written on

the blank edge of a newspaper. It was enclosed in a plastic baggie.

In a woman's handwriting, the note said,

Meet me at TCAAM shop after eight. We need to talk.

"It's not signed," I said.

"It doesn't need to be. What else can TCAAM mean but Two Cows And A Moose? This note had to be written by Emily Hargraves."

I couldn't believe that my dear friend was involved in Gabby's nephew's murder. "They dated for a while, Gabby. Everyone knows that. This could be from months ago."

"Turn the paper over," she demanded.

On the other side, I saw a date clearly printed on the paper.

It was the day Jude had been murdered.

"Have you shown this to anyone else?" I asked her.

"Who do you mean, the police?"

"Of course that's who I mean," I said.

"No, I just found it, so I came straight over here."

"How did you know that I would be here?" I asked.

"Come on, Suzanne. You're the only one in town who has a Jeep that color. Besides, where else would you be?"

I nodded as I stared at the note. "What do you expect me to do about this?"

Gabby frowned, took a deep breath, and then she said, "Suzanne, I know that you and Emily are close, but I need you to talk to her about what happened the night Jude was murdered. If she did it, I expect you to turn her in to the police, just like you've done with every other suspect you've found in the past."

I thought about it, and then I said, "You need to show this to Chief Martin," as I handed the note back to her. "You found it. It's your responsibility."

"I turned it over to you, though," Gabby said as she backed away from it as though it were radioactive. "If you think that's the right thing to do, then you need to handle it yourself."

"Why did you even *give* this to me?" I asked, feeling real anguish over the questions I was going to have to ask Emily if I decided to follow through on it.

"You're trying to find Jude's killer," Gabby said. "This might help."

"And you don't think that Chief Martin is trying to do the exact same thing?" I asked.

"Maybe, but we both know he's prone to pull the trigger as soon as he gets a solid suspect. I figured you could talk to Emily, bring this up, and then turn the note over to the police yourself."

"I don't know what I should do," I said, torn between loyalty to my friend and my duty to give the police any relevant information that I uncovered.

"Do whatever you want. Just don't destroy it."

"There's a copy, isn't there?" I asked.

Gabby just shrugged, but her grin told it all. She wasn't reckless enough to leave it in my hands entirely.

"The clock's ticking, Suzanne," she said, and then she headed back to ReNEWed, her shop beside Donut Hearts.

I still wasn't sure what I was going to do when I walked back into the Boxcar.

"Okay, I'm officially worried about you," Trish said the moment she saw my face. "What did that woman say to you?"

"Nothing," I said absently. I needed to move, and fast. "Has Grace ordered for us yet?"

"I just put it in, and I was getting ready to grab your teas. Why?"

"Can you cancel our order?" I asked.

"Not a problem. You're in trouble, aren't you, Suzanne?"

"I'm not, but one of my friends might be."

I motioned to Grace, who got up and came toward me.

Trish said, "One of these days I'm hoping that you'll explain to me what this was all about."

"I promise," I said. "Just not now."

Grace joined me up front. "What's going on?"

"We're leaving," I said.

"But I…"

"It's taken care of," I said.

I started for the door, and Grace turned back to wave to Trish. "It was fun. We simply must do it again sometime."

Trish just laughed, and Grace and I were out in the parking lot soon enough. I skipped picking up my Jeep, though. Where we were going was close enough to walk. I probably needed to get to the newsstand as quickly as I could, but I needed time to explain everything to Grace, too.

"What's the rush? Funny, but I don't smell smoke anywhere," she said as she tried to keep up with my agitated pace. "Is there a fire somewhere I don't know about?"

"Read this," I said as I handed her Emily's note to Jude.

Grace whistled as she read the front, so I added, "Now turn it over."

"Why did Gabby give this to you and not the police?" Grace asked me as she handed the baggied note back to me.

"Should I stop and call Chief Martin?" I asked as I stopped walking abruptly.

It took Grace a second to stop her forward progress as well. "No. You need to find out what this means yourself. Suzanne, Emily will tell you what's going on a long time before she'll tell the police. You need to handle this yourself. As a matter of fact, I don't even think that I should go in with you. This has to be between the two of you."

"We both know that Chief Martin is going to be

justifiably upset when I turn it over to him," I said.

"Maybe so, but if you can tell him what Emily says to you, it might just make up for it."

We were in front of the newsstand too soon for my taste. "So, you honestly believe that I should try to find out what happened first myself, right?" I asked.

"Go on. If any customers are inside, run 'em out. I'll stand guard out here so no one else can get in."

I didn't even question Grace about how she might do that. The woman had an imagination that could run circles around mine when she put her mind to it.

"Here goes nothing," I said as I took a deep breath and walked through the door.

At least no one else was inside but Emily.

"Suzanne, what a pleasant surprise," she said, and then she saw the expression on my face. "Or is it? Something's up, isn't it? Are you going to have to back out of making my wedding donuts?"

Wow, if that was the most serious problem she thought she had, Emily was in for a big surprise. "No, it's not that. Emily, we need to talk."

"Okay," she said. "I was about to lock up early so I could work on some wedding plans. Should I lock the door?"

"You can, but I've got Grace standing guard outside."

"This *is* serious," she said as she sat back on her stool by the register. The three stuffed animals—Cow, Spots, and Moose—were watching over us, and I could swear that the three of them were looking down on me with disapproval.

"Explain this to me," I said as I handed her the baggied note.

She didn't even have to read it, once she saw her own handwriting. I saw her frown deeply before she managed to suppress it. "Where did you get this?" she asked carefully.

"Do you recognize it?" I asked.

"Of course I do. It's my handwriting, after all. I don't have a clue who I wrote it to, though. It had to have been ages ago."

That sounded like a big fat lie to me. "Emily, it was discovered among Jude Williams's things today."

She bit her lower lip, and then Emily tried to laugh it off. "This? It's nothing. I must have written it a long time ago. Suzanne, you know that Jude and I used to go out. Why should it surprise anyone that I wrote him a note at one point asking him to meet me at my shop?"

"Turn it over and look at the date," I said as I tapped the note.

As she did, Emily's face went ashen. "It doesn't mean anything," she said as she threw it in the trash.

After I retrieved it, I said, "That's not the only copy, so getting rid of it wouldn't have done you any good." I softened my voice as I asked her, "Emily, what's going on here?"

She was trapped, and she knew it. "Suzanne, it's not what it looks like." She was begging me to believe her, but I had to harden my heart.

"Then tell me what it means," I said plainly.

Emily looked at me as though I'd just slapped her. "You think I killed him, don't you?"

"I don't know what to think," I said. "That's why I came here to see *you* instead of turning this incriminating evidence directly over to the police."

"Should I thank you for that?" Emily asked, snapping at me. "At least I expect *them* to doubt me."

"I'm just looking for answers," I said, wondering just how sound my reasoning had been for coming in there before turning the note over to the police chief. "Talk to me, Emily."

"I didn't do it," she said, her voice faltering. "Suzanne, you've got to believe me. Destroy that note, don't tell anyone about it, and I'll be forever in your debt. I'm begging you. Please."

"I can't," I said, the words nearly choking in my throat. "I'm not the only one who knows about this. It would make things a whole lot easier if you just came clean with me."

"I won't say another word to you," she said, her voice angry now. "Go ahead; do your worst. Call the police. I don't care. Only know one thing," she said as she looked hard into my eyes. "You are dead to me as of right now. Don't do anything for my wedding; don't even dare show your face. I might not be able to stop you from dirtying my name, but I don't have to stand here in my shop and listen to you browbeat me. Get out, Suzanne."

"Emily, it's not like that—"

"I said get out!"

I shook my head sadly and walked out the door. As I left, I heard the lock click in place behind me.

"Suzanne, I'm so sorry," Grace said as I rejoined her.

"Did you hear all of that?" I asked, still stunned by Emily's explosion.

"No offense, but it was kind of hard to miss. She didn't mean any of it," Grace said as she tried to comfort me.

"Funny, I got the impression that she meant every word of it," I said sadly.

"So, what are you going to do?"

"I'm doing what I promised her I'd do. I'm calling Chief Martin."

Grace took my hands in hers before I could reach for my cellphone. "Are you sure that's what you want to do?"

"Don't you start in on me, too," I said. "I made a promise, and I'm going to see it through, no matter what the consequences are."

"Okay. I support you, one hundred percent," she said.

I dialed the chief's number, and he answered on the

first ring. "Martin here," he said.

"Chief, I just found some important evidence you need to see. Meet me in front of my donut shop as soon as you can."

His voice had an edge to it as he asked, "Suzanne, have you been holding out on me?"

"Chief, I'm on the edge of a breakdown, and if you start yelling at me, too, I'm going to lose it. Please, no scolding; not today. I can't take it."

His voice was softer as he said, "I'll be there in two minutes."

As Grace and I started to walk down the street to Donut Hearts, neither one of us spoke a word. The chief caught up with us before we could get to my shop, and I quickly explained what Gabby had found, and my conversation with Emily about it, after I handed the note over to him.

"Anything else I should know?" he asked after I was finished.

"No, that's it."

"Thanks," he said, and then the police chief did a U-turn and headed back toward Two Cows and a Moose.

"What should we do now?" Grace asked me.

"I don't know about you, but I need a long hot shower and a nap."

"I imagine you'll fit a good cry in there somewhere too, won't you?" Grace asked softly.

"It wouldn't surprise me in the least," I said. "I've taken about all that I can take today."

"Drop me off at the house, then," she said. "Maybe we can get something to eat later tonight."

"Maybe," I said, "but I'm not making any promises."

"I understand," she said. Once I pulled into her drive, she got out, and then leaned in. "Suzanne, you're doing the best that anyone could do, given the circumstances."

"Then why do I feel like such a failure?" I asked her.

"It just comes with the territory, I guess," she said.

"Maybe so."

I drove the short distance home, hoping that Momma was gone. If I had to tell her what had happened with Emily, I didn't know how I was going to hold it together.

To my relief, she wasn't there.

It was time for that cleansing shower I'd promised myself. If there were any tears mixed in with the cascading water, there was no one there to see them but me, and I'm not going to say one way or the other. I felt a little better afterwards, and I slipped on my robe and lay down on my bed. I hadn't really planned on taking a nap, no matter what I'd told Grace, but evidently my body had other plans for me.

I woke up from my dreams as a giant hammer tried to slam me into the ground, and no matter how much I ran and tried to avoid it, it was about to crush me when I suddenly awoke.

It took me a few moments to realize that someone was outside, clearly trying to knock my front door down.

Chapter 13

I threw on some clothes and stumbled down the stairs.

As I opened the door, I asked loudly, "What's so urgent that you have to break my door down?"

Max frowned at me, and Peter had his back turned, looking out over the park that abutted our land. "Suzanne, we need to talk."

"Fine, then talk."

"Not out here," he said. "Inside."

Max might have changed in a great many ways, but that tone of voice hadn't. He might have been under the impression that it was a no-nonsense delivery, but it just made me dig my heels in. I brushed past him and sat on the porch swing. "You know what? You're not welcome in my home when you're acting like this."

"*Me*? What about you?" he asked accusingly.

"What *about* me?" I asked, and then I got it. "Oh. Emily came crying to you, didn't she?"

"Naturally, she told me what happened," Max said. "She wasn't crying about anything. Suzanne, did you really accuse her of killing Jude?"

"I asked her a question, and she lost it," I said.

"What was the question?" Peter asked. "Did you ask her if she killed Jude Williams?"

"No, that wasn't it," I said, and then I turned to Max. I was furious with Emily for turning to Max to rebuke me, but if there was any chance of friendship left between us, I wasn't going to be the one who told him that his fiancée had made a date before their wedding with her ex-boyfriend.

"What was it, then?" Peter asked. I didn't like the man on the best of days, and this clearly wasn't one of those.

"Don't you have somewhere else to be?"

He grinned at me. "No, ma'am. My job is to shadow the groom, and that's exactly what I'm doing."

"If there's even going to be a wedding now," Max said.

"She's not calling it off because of me, is she?" I asked.

"No, of course not. She doesn't want to get married when there's a cloud of murder over everything," Max said. He studied me for a few moments before he said softly, "I know the real question you asked her." He turned to Peter and said, "Wait for me by the car, would you?"

Peter looked astonished by the request. "I'm not going anywhere, buddy. You might need a witness."

"A witness to what, exactly?" I asked.

Peter just shrugged. "You never know."

"Fine, do what you want," Max said to him before he turned back to me. "I know that Emily met Jude the night he was murdered."

"What!" Peter said.

"Later," Max said to his best man before he turned back to me. "Suzanne, he was going to try to disrupt the wedding, so Emily thought it might not be a bad idea to confront him before he could. She met him, told him that even if I wasn't in the picture, she still wouldn't be interested in him, and that he should move on."

"And what did he say to that?" I asked.

"He didn't like it, but he finally accepted it," Max said.

"Did anyone witness this conversation but the two of them?" I asked.

"No, they were alone. Why?" Max asked.

"Then we can't exactly ask Jude if that's what *really* happened, now can we?"

"Suzanne, do you honestly think she killed him?"

I shook my head. "I don't want to, but it's something the police need to investigate. From the way Emily reacted to my questions, she seemed awfully guilty to me of something. If she didn't kill Jude, why did she react so violently when I asked her about the note? First she tried to deny it, and then she said it was from a long time ago. When I pointed out the date on back, she banned me from your wedding and fired me as the wedding donut caterer. She could have saved herself a lot of grief if she'd just told me the truth when I asked."

"She panicked, okay?" Max asked. "When you threatened to turn her in to the police, what was she supposed to do?"

"We've been friends for a very long time," I said.

"More than that once upon a time," he answered.

"I'm talking about Emily and me, not you and me, Max."

"Then shouldn't you have cut her a little slack?" he asked me.

"She should have trusted me," I said.

Max surprised me by nodding. "Yeah, maybe so, but she had a momentary lapse. She felt as though you were attacking her, and she reacted badly. She was really hurt when it felt as though you were accusing her of murder, Suzanne."

"What does she want from me, an apology? She's not going to get one, because like it or not, she belongs on my list."

"What list is that?" Peter asked me.

"My list of suspects," I said, staring straight at him.

"I suppose I'm on it, too, then," Peter said lightly.

"You had a fistfight with the man the night he died," I said. "How could you *not* be on everybody's list of suspects? I'm surprised Chief Martin let you leave the precinct."

"Sure, Jude and I fought, but I didn't kill him," Peter said.

"What was the fight about, anyway?"

"Not that it's any of your business, but I was doing the same thing that Emily was trying to do. I told him that if he showed up at the wedding, I'd make him live to regret it, and that's when he threw the first punch at me.

It wasn't the last one, either, but I got in a few good shots of my own. I might have hit him a few times, but I didn't kill him. Believe it or don't believe it. I'm past caring what you think."

"Do you really think that Peter should be a suspect on your list?" Max asked.

"As a matter of fact, I think that both of you are," I replied.

"Come on, Suzanne. Neither one of us killed him, and neither did Emily," Max said.

"So you say," I said. "While you're here, answer me this. Do either one of you have an alibi for the time of the murder?"

Max shrugged. "The police chief asked us the same thing. The only alibis we have are each other. We were in a hotel room in Charlotte having a little two-man bachelor party."

"Can the entertainment at least vouch for you? Come on, Max, don't try to deny that there were women there, too."

Max shook his head. "Nope, it was just the two of us. We shared a bottle of single malt whisky, a few really good cigars, and some old stories as we sat on a balcony overlooking the city lights."

"Just the two of you?" I asked, not believing him for one second.

"I'm marrying Emily," he said. "I don't want anybody else." He frowned, and then Max added, "That's not what this is really about, is it? Suzanne, you're not *jealous*, are you?"

I laughed in his face. "Believe me, I was done with you a long time ago."

"Then what is it?" Max asked. "Why come after Emily?"

"I'm not focusing solely on her, but I'm not giving her a free pass, either," I said. "I can't, not after I read that note."

"Then I'm afraid that Emily's not going to change her mind. I believe her one thousand percent. I'm really sorry, but if she doesn't want you at our wedding, I'm going to have to ask you to respect her wishes and not come."

"It's too bad that it's come to that, but I honestly don't have any choice." How had things gotten so out of hand so quickly?

"Come on, Peter. Let's go."

Peter saluted me as he walked off the porch, but Max didn't bother looking at me again.

After they drove away, I had to wonder who had initiated that little visit. Was Emily really expecting an apology from me after the way that she'd lied to me? She might just be overstressed because of the impending wedding, but that was no excuse to lie to me.

At least not unless she had something to hide.

As much as I hated it, there was nothing that I could do about it. I wasn't about to lie to Emily and tell her that everything was all right between us.

I'd just have to accept the fact that our friendship might just be more collateral damage from one of my unofficial murder investigations.

I walked back inside, still feeling pretty lousy and wondering where Momma was. I could use a little motherly comfort about now, but she was nowhere to be found. I discovered why when I walked into the kitchen. There was a note there from her, written in her precise hand.

Suzanne,
I'm meeting some old friends in Union Square tonight, so you're on your own for dinner. There are leftovers in the fridge!
Love You, Kiddo,
Momma

Great. She was deserting me in my time of need, just like everyone else. I was clearly in the mood to feel sorry for myself. I thought about calling Grace and asking her to join my little pity party when I suddenly knew who I wanted to call instead.

Jake had put me off long enough.

I dialed his number, fully expecting it to go straight to voicemail, but to my surprise, he answered immediately.

"Jake, what's going on with you? We need to talk, and I mean right now." I glanced at the clock in the kitchen before I added, "I can be there by nine, and I don't want to hear any more excuses about why it's not a good idea for me to drive three hours to talk to you face-to-face."

"Suzanne, there's no need for that," he said in a heavy voice.

"Oh, no. We're not having a conversation as important as this over the phone," I said.

"That's not the reason. I've been sitting in the park near your place for the past half hour working up the nerve to come to the house."

I looked outside. "I don't see you anywhere." Had he witnessed the confrontation between Peter, Max, and me?

"That's because I parked down the road. I can be there in thirty seconds if you still want to see me."

"Then I suggest you do get over here right now," I said, and then I hung up on him.

Running my fingers through my hair, I didn't have time to do much more to make myself presentable. Then again, why should I even bother even trying to do that? The chances were very good that I was about to be dumped, so I doubted that it mattered much what I looked like.

Jake drove up, but I stayed right where I was on the porch, sitting in the swing and trying not to look to anxious or eager.

"Hey," he said heavily as he got out and approached me.

"Hey," I replied.

He hesitated so long that I wondered if he'd temporarily lost the power of speech when he finally asked, "Could we walk around the park as we talk? It might make this a little easier to say."

Oh, great. This was it. I thought about being difficult about it, but finally I decided that I might as well give in. "Fine," I said as I got off the swing and walked down the steps toward him.

As we started walking together, I said, "You don't need to worry. I won't make a scene."

"Why not? This is pretty upsetting."

"I've had some time to deal with it," I said, though that wasn't entirely true. I couldn't imagine ever having enough time to get used to the fact that I was about to get dumped by the only man I'd really cared about since my marriage had fallen apart.

He looked at me with a confused expression on his face. "Suzanne, what are you talking about?"

"You're dumping me, aren't you?" I blurted out.

"No! Of course not! What gave you that idea?"

What was going on here? Had I misread all of the signals? "Come on, Jake. You've been really distracted, cold, and distant, not to mention impossible to get ahold of. Plus, you act like someone just shot your best friend every time that we talk lately."

"My feelings for you haven't changed," he said sadly.

"Then what is it? Why are you so glum?"

"I'm going to Alaska in four hours," he said, the words clearly weighing heavily on him.

"Is that all? Jake, that's not so bad. I understand that Alaska is wonderful this time of year. You'll have a great time on vacation."

"Suzanne, I'm not going on vacation. My services are

being loaned out to the Alaska State Police Department for the next twelve months. It's some kind of investigator's exchange program, and I wasn't given a choice in the matter."

"Is it because of the bombing?" I asked. Jake had turned down an assignment to guard the North Carolina governor, and his boss had taken the job instead. When there had been an attempt on the governor's life, Jake's boss had been wounded, though the governor himself had escaped unscathed.

"No, of course not. They tried to present this as a promotion, or at the very least a way to advance my career. I almost quit on the spot."

"Doesn't it sound like an adventure to you?" I asked.

"Maybe with *you*, but I don't want to leave you for a whole year," he said. Was that a tear crawling down his cheek?

"You have to do it, Jake. I'm sorry, but I won't have you turn something like this down because of me, let alone quit your job. A year's not that bad."

"It feels like a lifetime right now," he said. "Is there any chance that you'd go with me?"

I thought about leaving my donut shop behind for a year, leaving Grace, leaving my mother. I loved Jake, there was no doubt about that, but I couldn't just walk away from my life for him. I wasn't expecting a proposal, but it shocked me to the core when I realized that was the *only* way that I'd leave everything behind. Who knew? I turned out to be an old-fashioned gal after all.

I must have hesitated too long, because he answered the question for me. "I know. I felt ridiculous even asking you to leave everything for me."

"It's not that I don't love you, because I do," I said.

"I know that," he said, wiping away the tear I'd seen. "Forget I even asked. After all, you're right. What's a year, anyway? We'll be back together before you know it." He hesitated, and then Jake asked, "I can come back twice within the year's time, but if you could come up once, we'd only have to be apart three months at a time at the longest. Will you come visit me?"

"I promise," I said. "Jake, I'm so sorry," I added.

"Don't be," he answered. "We'll be fine. Well, I'd better get going."

"You just got here. Stay. Please."

"I would if I could, but there's just no time. I'm going to be pushed for time as it is. I love you, Suzanne."

"I love you, too," I said. "Can't you at least kiss me good-bye?"

He nodded, and then Jake took me in his arms. I did my best to breathe him in, to capture the essence of him to hold me over for the next few months, but it was impossible.

Finally, he broke free, and as he got into his car, ready to leave me for a year, I yelled out, "Call me when you get through security."

"Don't worry. That's not going to be a problem for me," he said, managing a feeble grin. "The job has some perks, after all."

"At least promise to call me when you get there, then," I said.

"I will. Good-bye, Suzanne."

"Bye," I said, and I stood there waving as he drove away.

He was really gone.

Why hadn't I said yes when he'd asked me to join him? Was I really that set in my ways that I couldn't do something that might ensure my future happiness? Was I afraid of what a commitment like that would mean to me? Or had I just been caught off guard by the suddenness of it all? I hadn't lost my boyfriend, at least not metaphorically.

I was still standing there looking out into the growing night when I heard footsteps approaching. Had Jake delayed his trip long enough to give me a proper farewell?

No.

It was Grace. She'd walked up from her house, and the second I saw her, I fell apart.

"Grace, I might have just made the biggest mistake in my life, and there's no way to fix it now."

She hugged me tightly, stroking my back lightly as she said, "It's okay, Suzanne. We'll figure out a way to make it all better."

I just wished that I believed her.

Jake was gone, and I was alone, by choice.

And I didn't see any way to make things right again.

Chapter 14

Two hours later, after a steady supply of sweet tea, homemade cookies, and apple pie, I was finally starting to feel a little better about my situation with Jake. Momma had come home an hour before, and she'd quickly joined in the support group. Both women kept reassuring me that they understood why I'd turned Jake's offer to join him down, but it still didn't help make me feel much better.

In the middle of a sentence, I yawned loudly, exhausted more from the emotion of the evening than any real weariness.

"Suzanne, look at the time. You'd better get off to bed right now if you're going to get *any* sleep tonight," Momma said.

"I could try, but I doubt that I'd sleep a wink," I said as I yawned again.

"You should at least make an attempt to get some rest," Grace added as she stood and stretched. "I've got a big day tomorrow myself."

"What's going on?" I asked, wondering if my friend might not be able to help me in my investigation the next day. I relied on Grace's company as well as her astute observations, and I hated the thought of digging deeper into Jude Williams's murder without her.

"I have a meeting in Hickory at eight, and another in Lenoir at nine, but I'll be back here by eleven," she said. "I promise."

"You don't have to rush back on my account," I said, though I didn't really mean it. "I know that your job is important to you."

"It is, but don't forget that I love these investigations just as much as you do." Grace hugged me again before she left, and then she said goodnight to my mother before she headed home.

Once Momma and I were alone, I asked her softly, "Tell me the truth. What would you have done in my shoes?"

"Suzanne, that's an impossible question to answer. What does your heart tell you?"

"Just that it's breaking," I answered.

She hugged me, and then Momma stroked my hair just as she'd done when I'd been a child. "There, there. It will all seem better in the morning."

"How can you be so sure?" I asked her.

"Time does more than wound all heels. It heals all wounds as well."

"Should I have gone?" I asked her again.

"Could you leave everything you have here behind to follow him?" she asked me softly.

"I don't know, but shouldn't I at least try?"

"My dear child, why don't you think about it for a week and see how you feel once the shock of Jake's departure eases a bit? You're in no position to make a rational decision tonight. Don't you think that Jake must have realized that himself? After all, from the sound of it, he didn't push you very hard to go with him, did he?"

"No, and that worries me a little, too. If he'd wanted me with him, why did he ask me just once?"

Momma shook her head. "The ways of men are just as mysterious to us as our ways are to them. It might be that he was afraid to ask you in the first place, and asking twice might have seemed like he was begging. Now answer me this honestly. Does that seem like something Jake Bishop would do, no matter how much his own heart might be breaking?"

"No, you're right," I said, suddenly feeling better because Jake could just possibly be as miserable as I was right now. I knew that it was petty of me, but I couldn't help it. "If you don't mind, I think I *will* try to get some sleep. Thanks for everything tonight."

"Grace had things well in hand before I got here," she said. "I'm not sure that I added all that much in the end."

"That's where you're wrong. When a girl's heart is broken, she needs her mother most of all."

Momma's smile was full as she said, "Then I'm glad that I could be here for you. If you want to talk, even if it's the middle of the night, wake me. Will you do that for me?"

"I promise," I said. "Good night."

"Good night, Suzanne."

I was just about to go to sleep when my cellphone rang.

It was Jake.

"Suzanne, I'm so sorry that I sprang that on you at the last second. I can be such an idiot sometimes. Can you forgive me?"

I laughed, just happy to hear his voice again. "Only if you forgive me for not dropping everything and flying off to Alaska with you."

"You're much too practical for that," he said. "I should never have put you in that position in the first place. I guess it was pretty cowardly of me."

This from a man who faced down armed criminals on a regular basis. "Jake, you are many things, but cowardly isn't one of them."

"Oh, I can stand my share of danger, but I should have handled this entire mess better than I have."

"Tell you what. Let's give each other a free pass and stop beating ourselves up about it, okay? It's not like we can't see each other more often than every three months, and we can talk on the phone every day."

He laughed. "We don't talk that often now."

"Maybe not. I hope you have a safe flight. Call me when you land, okay?"

"No matter what time it is?" he asked.

"Chances are that I'll either be making donuts or selling them," I said. "Don't worry about waking me up."

"Thanks, Suzanne. I can't believe how lucky I was to find you."

"It was part of another murder investigation, if you remember."

"I'm not about to forget," he said. "Speaking of murder, I hear you're in the thick of another one."

"How did you hear that?" I asked.

"Chief Martin called me the day before yesterday," Jake admitted. "Don't tell him that I told you so, but he asked me to keep an eye on you."

"Is he worried about me?" I asked.

"He worries about everything. The man honestly cares for you."

"Because of Momma," I said.

"There's always that, but I think he likes your spunk, too."

"How about you?"

"I like it just fine," Jake said. I could hear speakers in the background of the airport making an announcement, and he added quickly, "I've got to run. I'll talk to you soon."

"Have a safe flight, Jake. I love you."

"I love you, too."

When we hung up, I felt a great deal better than I had all day. Talking it out with Momma and Grace had given me a little perspective, but working things out with Jake was even more important to me. He had said farewell in a much better way, not a final good-bye, and we were in as good a place as we could be, given the circumstances. We'd work things out one way or the other, I was sure about that, but I was going to stop feeling sorry for myself because he was a continent away. Others had gone through much worse to be together and it had all worked out fine in the end, so there was no reason to think that we would end up otherwise. In the meantime, I had a renewed interest in catching a killer, and I wasn't going to be able to do it without sleep. I climbed into bed and fell asleep, wrapped in my boyfriend's love and finally understanding that though distance separated our bodies, our hearts were together, and that was really all that counted.

Chapter 15

"Good morning, Suzanne," Emma said the next day as she walked into Donut Hearts.

I glanced up at the clock before I answered her. "You're early today." I hadn't even finished the batter for all of my cake donuts yet. Usually I was icing the last batch of them when Emma came in. "What's the matter? Couldn't sleep?"

"Actually, I need to talk to you," Emma said solemnly.

"Oh, no. You're not quitting again, are you?" My assistant had left for college once before, but she'd come back soon enough when living away from home hadn't suited her.

"No, of course not," she said.

"Then what do you want to talk about?"

"I spoke with Emily last night," she said tentatively.

"I'm not surprised. You two are best friends, after all."

"That's the thing," Emma said softly. "She asked me to take over for you."

"*You're* going to make the wedding donuts now?" I asked before I quickly added, "Not that you wouldn't be perfectly capable of doing it. It just surprises me, that's all."

"I'm not making donuts *or* a cake," Emma said. "Her mother's got that covered. I'm standing in as her maid of honor. At least I will if you give me your blessing. I told Emily that I wouldn't do it if you had a problem with it. She's just going to have to find someone else."

"Of course I don't mind," I said. "Emma, I'm happy for you. You know, you should have had the job from the start. I just got it because of my interfering."

"I'm so sorry about this rift between you and Emily. Are you really not even coming to the wedding?" Emma asked.

"She told me not to come, and I'm going to respect her wishes," I said.

In a soft voice, my assistant said, "All you have to do is apologize."

That was something that I wasn't about to do. "Emma, it might be better for both our sakes if we both just drop this, okay? I don't want my problems I might have with Emily to bleed over into *our* relationship."

"I don't want that, either," she said quickly. "Are *we* still good?"

"We're perfectly fine," I said as I forced a smile.

"Then there's only one other thing I'd like to talk to you about," Emma said as I worked on the batter for our pumpkin donuts. It was getting to be that time of year again, and I always enjoyed the smell of the frying donuts.

"Does it involve Emily?" I asked.

"Not directly. It *is* about Jude's murder, though. If you don't want to talk about it, I understand completely, but Dad came across something that I thought you might like to know."

Emma's father was constantly trying to turn his newspaper into something more than a place just for ads and comics. "Are you sure you won't be breaking any confidences with him by telling me?"

"I asked him that, and he gave me his blessing." Emma looked at the clock as she added with a smile, "It doesn't make too much difference, since the paper will be out by six AM. He figured you weren't going to tell anybody until we opened, anyway. Could you do that much for me?"

"Sure thing," I said. "So tell me, what's the big news?"

"Dad found out the reason behind the fight Peter had with Jude the night he died, and he's going to publish it today."

"That's old news," I said as I went back to the batter.

"Peter told me himself that he was trying to persuade Jude not to crash the wedding. Evidently they had words about it, and it led to a fistfight."

"He lied to you, Suzanne," Emma said. "That wasn't the real reason at all."

"Okay, you've got my attention," I said as I set the batter aside. "Why did the two of them fight, if it wasn't about the wedding?"

"Dad believes that both men were dating the same woman," Emma said smugly.

"Does he know who it is?" I asked, trying not to give anything away. Could Peter have been going out with Lisa Grambling, too? I certainly had something else to ask her about the next time I saw her.

"No, he's calling her Madam X for now. He's even got a shadow outline of a woman to go along with the article. It sounds like a real winner."

Ray Blake had been known to run with far less, and most folks discounted his supposed exposés with grains of salt. I had a hunch that Ray was off base on this one as well. After all, Peter wasn't all that familiar with April Springs. How could he have even met Lisa? "Is that all he's got?" I asked.

"No, there's more. Jude owed someone in town a fair amount of money, and Dad thinks that might also be a reason that he was murdered, not out of jealousy."

"That's interesting. I suppose he's calling him Mister X," I said with a smile.

"Dad isn't naming him in the paper because he doesn't want to take a chance on getting sued, but he's pretty sure who it is. Can you keep a secret?" she asked me.

More than she knew. I wasn't all that excited about her confiding in me, though. "Are you sure that you're at liberty to tell me everything?" I asked.

"I know that you won't spread it around. It's Frank Grambling."

My shock must have shown on my face. "Frank?

Seriously?" If Ray Blake was right, which was a mighty big if, then Jude was not only sleeping with the man's wife but stealing money from him as well. Frank had just managed to climb a few notches higher on my list if it were true.

Emma couldn't hide her smile. "I know; can you believe it? Jude sold Frank some gold that turned out to be fake. When Frank demanded his money back, Jude told him that the cash was already gone and that Frank should just forget about it. I don't know how well you know Frank Grambling, but Dad said that was something he wasn't about to do. He's going to dig the truth out, and he's hoping that by running this story, Frank will come clean and admit what he's done."

"That's a lot to hope for," I said. "If he has any real proof, he should tell Chief Martin." I fully realized how that sounded since I'd been known to delay handing over shaky evidence myself in the past.

"Nope. Dad says that real journalists don't do that."

"Is he willing to go to jail over it?" I asked.

"Are you kidding? There's nothing he'd like better! He's already got the headline. *Journalist Jailed; Won't Talk.*"

"Well, then for his sake, I hope he's sitting in jail behind bars by nightfall."

Emma laughed. "I'm going to tell him that you said that."

"Be my guest," I said. "Now, if we're finished speculating, you need to go set up the dining room so I can drop these donuts into the fryer."

She left as I forced the batter into our heavy steel dropper and began making perfect little rings of goodness in the hot oil. Two minutes later, I took my chopsticks and turned them once, revealing a dark golden side of each treat. After they cooked on that side, I pulled them out and poured icing over them all, watching as the glaze crystalized and formed perfect, delightful coatings. Once I was finished, I called Emma back in.

"Are you ready to get started on the dishes?" I asked.

"I can't wait," she said. As I mixed the yeast dough, we chatted about the weather and a certain real estate agent in town named Larry Evans who was rumored to be wooing four different women in April Springs. It was outrageous, and nobody really believed it, but it was entertaining. The fact that the agent was in his eighties just helped add to the delight of me thinking of him slipping from one bedroom in town to another. I didn't doubt that there was some basis to the rumor. I'd seen the way Larry had eyed me when he'd come into the shop. The man was a wolf in a green blazer, the jacket of choice for all of the agents in his firm.

The yeast dough was mixed soon enough, and as we waited for it to rest and raise, Emma and I took our standard break. At least we started to, but then my cellphone rang, and I knew exactly who was calling me that early in the morning.

"Jake, are you there already?" I asked.

"No," he said, out of breath. I could hear him running and terminal sounds all around him. "Our flight was late, and I've got to run to catch my next one. Fortunately my flight's going through Vegas. The terminal's not that big, so I'm going to a nearby gate."

"You won't even have time to drop a quarter in the slot machine, will you?" I asked. Grace had gone to Las Vegas after winning a sales contest for her company, and she'd marveled that they even allowed gambling in the airport after she got through security.

"I don't gamble," he said. "Just wanted to say hi while I had the chance. Hi."

"Hi yourself. Call me when you get there, will you?"

"Promise," he said. "Love you."

"I love you, too," I said as he hung up.

Emma was standing there grinning at me when I hung

up. "That's an early phone call, even for you, Suzanne. Do I even have to ask who it was?"

"No, you sure don't."

"It didn't last long," she said.

"He was changing planes, so he couldn't chat."

"Oh, that sounds exciting. Where's he going?" Emma asked me.

"Alaska," I said, my heart sinking a little as I said it.

"Wow; that's a long way from North Carolina," she said. "Will he be back soon?"

I didn't want to get into that with her, but I really didn't have much choice. It was just the two of us, and we'd already banned talking about Emily's wedding. "In a few months," I said.

"That long?"

"That's just to visit. He'll be working there for a year, but before you say a word, I don't want to talk about that, either."

Emma nodded. "We sure are limiting our topics of conversation lately, aren't we?" she asked me with a grin.

"Well, there's always Larry," I said, smiling.

"Yes, we'll always have Larry."

Chapter 16

I was surprised to see our mayor waiting out front when I unlocked the front door promptly at six AM. "Come on in, George," I said as I stepped aside to let him pass. "What brings you out so early today?"

"I'm usually up before this," the mayor said as he took his jacket off and hung it on the rack.

"Maybe so, but you don't often get donuts first thing," I said. "What's going on? Is Polly out of town?" Polly North was George's secretary, and also his girlfriend, though he would never come out and admit it. George thought it was a ridiculous name for a woman he was seeing, but he hadn't liked any of my other choices, either, so we were stuck with it.

"As a matter of fact, she's in Wilmington. One of her kids is having a baby, so she went to help out."

"Wow, that's some kind of mom," I said.

"I'm sure that your mother would do the same thing for you," George said.

"I'm not pregnant, though." I pretended to study my belly. "Do I look pregnant? George, are you saying that if I'm not pregnant, I'm getting fat?"

"What? No. Of course not. I'd never say any such thing."

He stopped when he saw my grin. "You're too easy to tease, my friend. It's not even any fun anymore."

As he fought his blush, the mayor said, "You could always stop doing it, then."

"Not on your life," I said and kissed his cheek lightly, an act that made his face burn even brighter. "Let me get you coffee and a donut on the house," I said as I walked to the counter.

"You used to just do that when I was working on a case with you," George said as he took a stool. "Between the two of us, I miss those days."

"I do, too, but you're serving the greater good right where you are now."

He laughed without joy. "Funny, it feels as though I mostly preside over meetings where everyone involved acts as though they were still in junior high school. Sometimes I'd like to take the lot of them over my knee and teach them about discipline."

"I'm afraid you'd get arrested if you did that," I said as I poured him a cup of coffee and grabbed a plain cake donut for him.

"Maybe so, but I bet I'd be reelected in a landslide if I showed that bunch some discipline." He took a sip of coffee, smiled, and then he added, "Not that I want this crazy job again."

"Aren't you going to run for reelection?" I asked. My mother had basically tricked George into becoming mayor, but he was the best one that we'd ever had, and I for one would hate to lose him.

"I don't know. It's too soon to say."

"George, your term is about up. Surely you've got to make up your mind soon one way or the other."

"You're starting to sound like Polly now," he said then took a bite of donut.

"Does she want you to run again?"

"So she says. Personally, I think that she should run herself. She does most of the work now anyway; she might as well have the title and the fancy office that goes along with it."

"Did you suggest that to her?" I asked him.

"I did, and she laughed for three solid minutes before she could get her breath again. She claimed that she enjoyed being the power behind the throne, but I know better. She's too smart to ever run for mayor."

"Then I guess you're stuck with it," I said with a grin. Things were quiet so far, and though I would have liked having more business, it was nice being able to spend time with my old friend.

"Maybe so, but don't forget, you've got a sharp detective's mind right here at your disposal," he said as he tapped his temple with a thick and meaty finger. "Say, for instance, you'd like to talk about Jude Williams' murder case with someone with experience in investigating homicides, you wouldn't have to go far."

"Don't offer unless you're willing to let me take you up on it," I said.

"Suzanne, nothing would make me happier," he said.

We were still alone, and Emma was in back washing dishes. There was no doubt in my mind that her music was cranked up to a volume high enough to completely block out our conversation.

"Okay, here goes," I said, and I started to bring him up to date on what Grace and I had learned so far.

After I listed my suspects and my reasons for suspecting them, George whistled softly under his breath. "Wow, I didn't realize so many people around here had a reason to kill Jude Williams. The chief must be going crazy tracking down leads."

"I haven't seen much of him lately," I admitted. "Momma hasn't, either, so you *know* he must be busy."

"I wonder how your two lists compare," George said.

"We'll probably never know, since we don't always compare notes."

George looked surprised by that. "I thought that you two had hammered out some kind of way to investigate without stepping on each other's toes."

"What makes you think that?" I asked him.

"Isn't it true?"

"That's beside the point. Have you been keeping tabs on me, George?"

He shrugged. "I might have asked a question or two around the precinct," he admitted. When he saw me staring at him, George was quick to add, "Suzanne, are you really all that surprised?"

"No," I said, and then added a laugh. "You just can't

help yourself, can you?"

"Apparently not. So, where do you go from here?"

"Grace and I are going to keep digging until we uncover something that points toward a killer."

"And you're sure that you don't need my help?" George asked.

"Don't you have your hands full running April Springs?"

He scratched his chin. "Ordinarily I'd say that it runs itself, but with Polly gone, I'm up to my eyebrows in work. I don't know how she does it."

"Maybe you should give her a raise when she gets back," I suggested.

"Maybe you're right."

"So, do you have any advice for me, George?"

"Just be careful, Suzanne. There's a killer on that list of yours; you can be sure of it. I wouldn't be alone with any of them, and that includes Gabby."

"Do you honestly think that she might have killed her own nephew?" I asked. I couldn't fathom the circumstances that it could be true. I knew Gabby, and she wasn't a killer.

"If folks knew how many homicides were committed by family members, they'd never be able to sleep at night," he said.

"Okay. I'll be careful."

"And not just around Gabby. You need to watch your back with all of them, including Max."

I was surprised yet again. "There you're way off base, George. My ex-husband is many things, but he's no murderer. I would swear to that under oath."

"Suzanne, what does Max want more than anything in the world right now?" George asked me.

I didn't even have to think about it. "He wants to marry Emily." It didn't bother me to say it. I was well and truly over my ex-husband, and as a matter of fact, I was happy that he'd been able to find someone he cared about the way that I cared about Jake.

"And what would he do if someone tried to stop that from happening? Don't answer me; just think about it," George said as he finished his donut and emptied his coffee.

"I honestly don't know. I suppose it depended on how desperate he was."

"That a girl. Now you're thinking like a cop."

"I sure hope not," I said. "No offense intended."

"None taken," the mayor said with a shrug. "Out of curiosity, why would that be such a bad thing?"

"The police are already working on the case. The only thing I bring to the table is coming at the investigation from a completely different perspective. If I lose that, then I'm going to stop investigating murder and leave it to the professionals."

"What are the odds of that happening?" he asked with a grin.

"Not very good," I admitted. "How about another donut and a refill?" I asked him as I reached for the coffee pot.

"I'd better not," he said as he patted his stomach.

"I'm impressed," I said as I put the coffee pot back.

"Don't be. I promised Polly that I'd behave myself, so I'm going to fight off all of the temptation that comes my way."

"That doesn't sound like much fun," I replied with a smile.

"It's just the price I pay for being so virtuous," he said as he grinned at me.

As he pulled out his wallet, I reminded him, "It's my treat, remember?"

"But I didn't help you," he protested.

"Nonsense. I asked for some advice, and you gave it to me. Fair is fair."

"At least let me leave you a tip," he said.

"No, sorry; that's part of the deal."

"Fine, have it your way," George said as he put his wallet back in his pocket.

"Any final words of direction before you go?" I asked him as I walked him to the door.

"Yes. I'd focus on Reggie if I were you."

"Not Frank?" I asked, surprised by the advice. "It sounds as though he has more motive than anyone else. Don't you think that if Reggie were going to do something to avenge his daughter, he would have done it by now?"

"Not necessarily. Seeing Jude again could have brought everything back for him, all of the pain that he's suffered over the years. It's been my experience that people sometimes snap years later, but the devastation is just the same. He lost his daughter, and he blamed Jude for it. There's no stronger motive as far as I'm concerned."

"Okay," I said. "I'll keep him in mind."

"Do that. One more thing, Suzanne."

"Yes?" He looked a little embarrassed by what he had to say next.

After ten seconds, I said, "George, we've been friends too long for you to pull any punches. What's going on?"

"I wasn't supposed to say anything, but Jake called me last night."

That was odd. "What did he have to say?"

"He told me that he had to take this Alaska assignment, and then he asked me to keep an eye out for you."

"So, this morning wasn't *just* about my donuts?" I asked. It was sweet of Jake to worry about me, but I was a big girl, used to taking care of myself. I wasn't exactly sure how I felt about him lining up reinforcements for me, but I knew that he was motivated by his love for me, so I decided to accept the gesture for what it was.

"Suzanne, it's *always* your donuts," George said with

a smile, obviously relieved that I hadn't exploded. "The advice was just extra."

I kissed him on the cheek again. That was getting to be a habit lately, but I hoped that George didn't mind.

"What was that for?" he asked.

"For telling me the truth," I said.

"You won't mention this conversation to Jake, will you?" he asked.

"No. We'll consider it our little secret."

"I appreciate that. I've got a real fondness for that boyfriend of yours."

"I do, too," I said with a smile.

"I should hope so," George said. He added in a more serious voice, "It will all work out, Suzanne. You just have to have faith."

"Thank you," I said.

After George was gone, I thought about all that he'd said to me, but nothing rang truer than his last bit of advice. I was determined to keep Jake in my life as long as he wanted to be there, no matter how far away he might be.

Chapter 17

Ten minutes before we were due to close, Chief Martin walked into the donut shop. He'd finally taken a break with his diet, and he'd even had a single donut twice in the past month, but I knew better than to think that he was off the diet wagon completely. Personally, I was glad that he'd stopped losing weight. I was actually starting to get worried about him.

"Care for some coffee, or is this an official visit?" I asked him with a slight smile. There were a few customers in the shop, and I noticed a few of them perk up to hear the answer to my question.

"Nothing official. I just had a craving for a lemon-filled donut. Do you happen to have any left?"

I checked the racks, and I found one last donut that fit the bill. "You're in luck. Would you like some coffee, too?" I asked.

"Why not?" he asked.

I noticed that we'd quickly lost the attention of my customers as they went back to their own conversations. I knew from experience that the rumor mill in April Springs was alive and well, but for once, I was glad not to be a subject of gossip around town.

As I got him his donut and coffee, he sat down in the seat George had occupied nearly five hours before. I was suddenly getting a lot of attention, and I couldn't help but wonder if their visits were related. "Did Jake call you last night by any chance?"

"Why would he?" the chief asked as he took a small bite of his donut.

"Has the mayor called you, then?" I asked.

The chief put his donut back down. "Suzanne, what have you been up to?"

"Me? Nothing. At least nothing that you don't

already know about. Why do you ask?"

"First you want to know if Jake called me, and then you ask me about the mayor. It sounds to me as though you're up to something."

"Yeah, I can see that," I said with a smile. "Sorry."

"That's okay," he said. "How are you holding up?" he asked in a softer voice.

"I'm a little bit tired, but that's to be expected. I'm about to end a long shift on my feet."

"That's not what I meant," he said. "Don't worry. It will be fine."

"I'm going to kill my mother," I said as I put it together and reached for my cellphone.

"Hang on a second," Chief Martin said, clearly alarmed by my threat. "Why would you do that?"

"She obviously told you that Jake was gone," I said. "I can't believe that she'd do such a thing."

"She didn't," the chief said plainly.

As I put my cellphone back in my jeans, I asked, "Then who did?"

"I really can't say," he answered.

"It was Jake," I said.

"I never said that."

"No, but you didn't deny it. Why did you just lie to me?" I asked him, unhappy with this conversation in general.

"I never lied," he said.

"I asked you if Jake called you," I said loudly. We were getting some attention again, but I didn't care at that point.

"And I asked you why would he? Suzanne, I never lied to you."

"You avoided the question completely, though, didn't you?"

"Gosh, it's a good thing you've never done that with me," the police chief said with a smile.

I wanted to feel a little righteous indignation, but I

couldn't muster any up, especially since he was dead right about me. I smiled back at him. "Point well taken. Now that we've got that settled, let's just assume that Jake called you and asked you to keep an eye on me while he was gone."

He nodded as he said, "I'm sorry, but I can't confirm or deny that."

"Got it. I'm fine, by the way. Thanks for checking up on me. How's your investigation going?"

"We're muddling through. And you?" he asked as he took a sip of coffee. Two small bites of donut were gone, but the majority of it was still there on his plate.

"It's slow going, but then I don't have to tell you that." I gestured to his plate. "Is something wrong with that donut?"

"No, it's delicious. I'd just better not eat the whole thing."

"Go on, live a little," I said with a grin.

"That is exactly how I ended up bursting out of my uniform in the first place," he said as he pushed the plate away.

I got rid of it so it wouldn't tempt him anymore. "I wish I had your willpower," I said.

"I have the best incentive in the world," he said.

"What's that? Would you care to share?"

"Can't you guess?" he asked.

"Momma," I answered.

"Bingo." After taking another sip of coffee, he asked softly, "Is your list as long as mine is?"

"I don't know. Are we sharing again?" I asked him.

"I wouldn't mind hearing about who are suspects in your mind," he said.

Okay, the chief was ready to play again, and who was I to say no? I took a napkin from the nearest holder and pulled out my pen. In a hasty scrawl, I wrote the names REGGIE NANCE, FRANK GRAMBLING, LISA GRAMBLING, MAX, PETER, GABBY, and finally, a little reluctantly, I added, EMILY.

After I slid it across the counter to him, he took it and studied it for a few seconds. "Wow, that's longer than my list, and I thought I had *everybody* down."

"Have you eliminated any of mine yet?" I asked him.

"No, but I'm close to wiping three or four names off your list," he said. The chief looked at me a second, and then he added, "I can't say which ones at the moment. I'm sorry."

"It's fine. I understand. You're running an official police investigation here. Could you at least tell me the names I can cross off when you find that they aren't viable suspects anymore? That alone would be a big help."

"I can do that," he said. "Mind if I keep this?" he asked as he held the napkin up.

"Be my guest," I said, and he folded it up and then tucked it into his shirt pocket.

As he slid a five across the counter toward me, I thought about comping him just as I had George, but I knew that the police chief a hard and fast rule about freebies, so I just thanked him and gave him his change.

"Thanks for stopping by," I said.

"Happy to do it," the police chief answered, and then he left.

It appeared that Jake had done his best to make sure that I had support while he was away.

It really hadn't been all that shocking. After all, I knew that he loved me, and I loved him right back.

The question was, why was I still in April Springs while he was in Alaska? Wasn't that where I needed to be instead of trying to solve a murder so far away?

Maybe, just maybe, I'd made the wrong decision turning down Jake's offer to go with him. I needed to give some serious thought about my future and the possibility that it might be away from April Springs. It would mean selling the donut shop and leaving my family and friends far behind, but if I wasn't willing to do it all for love, could it really be *called* love? I cherished my work, my mother, and my friends. Could I give it all up to be with Jake?

Should I?

At the moment, I had no idea.

"Are we going to close up soon?" Emma asked me a little later, pulling me out of my thoughts.

"What?" I asked. "What time is it?" I answered my own question when I looked at the clock and saw that it was seven minutes after eleven. "Sorry, I must have zoned out." I turned to the two remaining customers and added, "We're closed, folks. Thanks for coming in."

After everyone was gone, I locked the door and flipped the sign. "How are the dishes coming?" I asked Emma.

"They're done, and the last few donuts are all boxed up. Suzanne, are you okay?"

"I'm fine," I said, "but thanks for asking. If the kitchen's clean, you can take off."

"I don't mind staying and helping you with the front," she said as she grabbed a rag.

"Okay, if you're sure. Thanks."

As Emma wiped the tables down and swept the front, I worked on closing out the register. We balanced out, always a nice result, and I let Emma out.

"Aren't you coming?" she asked.

"No, I'm waiting for Grace," I said.

"I can wait with you, if you'd like me to."

I took Emma's hands in mine. "I'm fine. I promise. Now scoot. Don't you have a class this afternoon?"

"Don't remind me," she said with a grimace. "I'm not a big fan of higher mathematics."

"Sorry I can't help you, but I can barely balance the day's receipts," I said.

"I'm off then, if you're sure."

"Absolutely," I said.

After she was gone, I locked the door behind her and sat down on one of our most comfortable sofas. If I didn't hear from Grace by eleven thirty, I was going to call her. I wasn't normally so concerned about her whereabouts, but when we were investigating a murder, it was a different matter entirely. I watched the minute hand as it crept downward, and I was about to take out my cellphone when she rushed up to the donut shop.

I unlocked the door, stepped outside with my deposit and my donuts, and then I locked it back behind me.

"Sorry I'm late," she said, nearly out of breath. "I didn't think my last meeting would ever end."

"You're fine," I said. "After we swing by the bank, why don't we grab a bite to eat before we start investigating? I'm starved."

"That sounds good to me. I overslept and missed breakfast."

"Want a donut?" I asked her as I extended the box to her.

"Don't tempt me," she said, and after a moment's pause, she lifted the lid. "Maybe I'll have a nibble until we get to the Boxcar."

I laughed as I pointed across the street. "You can't wait that long? You must be starving."

"Sure I could wait, but why would I?" she asked with a grin as she chose two blueberry donut holes. "There, I'm good now."

"Are you telling me that you're too full to have lunch now?"

"You're kidding, right? That was just to take the edge off," Grace said as she wiped her hands on a tissue she dug out of her purse.

When we got to the Boxcar, Trish eyed the box in my hand. "Suzanne, did you bring me a present for my birthday?"

"Is it your birthday?" I asked. "Happy birthday,

Trish."

There were a few more well wishes from nearby customers when Trish said, "Before you all burst out in song, it is not, I repeat, not my birthday."

"Then why did you say it was?" a nearby customer asked.

"Am I going to have trouble with you, Cliff?"

"No, ma'am," Cliff said quickly. "No trouble at all."

"Good," Trish said before she turned back to us. "I have to keep my eye on him constantly," she said with a smile. "Now, are those for me?"

"They are," I said as I held the box forward.

"Even though it's not my birthday?"

"Even then," I said.

"Excellent," she said as she took the box and lifted the lid. "Wow, these look fantastic. You shouldn't have, but I'm really glad that you did." She slid the box under the cash register station and then waved a hand toward the diner. "Sit wherever you'd like."

Grace and I found an empty table in back and jumped on it before anyone else could. Trish's diner was a popular destination for folks in April Springs, and it was always nice to be able to find a table, though never guaranteed.

"Now before I get my hopes up, we're actually going to get to *eat* this meal, right?" Grace asked.

"I'm not making any promises," I said with a grin, "but I think we're good."

"Excellent," Grace said as Trish approached the table with two sweet teas.

"I thought I'd go ahead and get you started, just in case you two are short on time."

"Did you already put our order in, too, Trish?" I asked as I laughed.

"Two burgers and fries. Was that wrong of me?" she asked.

I looked at Grace, who smiled back at me as she

nodded. "Sold."

"Good. I knew that I could count on you both."

"I'm not sure how much of a good thing it is that we're so predictable," Grace said. "We might lose our reputations for being mysterious and inscrutable."

"Your secrets are safe with me," Trish said. She glanced over and saw Rick Westwood standing at the register and looking impatient.

"I'll be right there, Rick," she said to him.

"I don't have all day, Trish," Rick said in exasperation.

"Tell you what. Today's meal is on me," she said.

Rick knew her too well not to recognize a trap when he saw one. "What's the catch?"

"Next time you come in, you pay whatever I decide is right," she replied.

Rick seemed to think about it for a second, and then he answered, "On second thought, I'm not in any hurry at all. You be sure to take all of the time that you need."

Trish's grin was infectious. "Wow, what a good decision that was."

I said, "You're terrible; you know that, don't you?"

"He loves it, and so did everyone else in earshot. If I ran every time somebody wanted me to, I wouldn't have a second's peace."

"Maybe so," I said, "but I couldn't get away with that at the donut shop."

"You never know until you try," Trish said.

"I don't have your guts," I replied.

"That's not it. You're plenty brave enough. I think it's that you don't want to lose any customers."

"And you're not afraid of that?" Grace asked.

She laughed. "Where is Rick Westwood going to have lunch if he doesn't come here? He's sure not going to grill up his own hamburger at home."

"You sound pretty sure of yourself," Grace said.

"I'm sure enough." She glanced back at Rick, who

was standing patiently there and not making any eye contact with Trish at all. It appeared that he was just passing the time of day as he stood patiently at the register. The fact that he had a ten in his hand and one of Trish's bills in the other didn't even seem to be a factor.

"I suppose I've made him wait long enough," Trish said. In a lower voice, she added, "He did a good job waiting. Maybe I'll give him a discount."

"Won't that ruin your reputation for being tough?" I asked her.

"Do you honestly think he'd have the nerve to tell anybody?" she asked with a laugh. "Your food will be out soon."

We both watched her walk up front to the register and take care of Rick. After he was gone, Grace turned to me and asked, "Any ideas about which suspect we should talk to first?"

"It's a toss-up in my book. I'm leaning toward Frank, but George thinks that we should focus on Reggie Nance instead."

Grace looked surprised. "Since when did George start consulting with us again?"

"It wasn't like that," I explained. "He came by to check up on me, and while he was here, we discussed the case."

"Why would he check up on you?"

"I'll give you three guesses," I told her, and then I took a sip of sweet tea. It was cold, rich, and sugary enough to put me in a diabetic coma; in other words, it was perfect.

"*Jake* called him?" Grace asked.

"You got it in one," I said.

She studied me for a few seconds. "You don't look all that upset by it."

"He's just looking out for me. What can I say? I must be lovable."

Grace pretended to look me up and down. "I don't know. I don't see it myself."

I gave her a playful shove. "That's because you're not looking hard enough. So, which man should we tackle first?"

"Suzanne, I hate to go against your instincts, but if George thinks that we should look hard at Reggie, I for one would like to know why. We can talk to Frank after we grill Reggie."

"I have no problem with that at all," I said as Trish suddenly appeared carrying two heavily laden plates our way. "Looks like lunch is on the way."

"Excellent," Grace said with a smile. "I'm so hungry I could eat both orders."

"But you'd never do that to me, would you?" I asked her.

"No."

"And why exactly is that?"

She grinned before answering. "Because I know that if I tried, I'd probably lose a hand."

"I'm not that harsh. It might just be a finger."

She pretended to think it over before she answered. "I still don't think I want to take the chance."

"Wise, my friend; very wise."

"Dig in and enjoy," Trish said as she put the plates down.

Grace and I did exactly as we were told, enjoying the sheer decadence of Trish's food. I'd have to cut back on something soon or I'd never fit into my jeans again, but it would have to be something besides the Boxcar's food.

It was just too good.

We were up front paying when my cellphone rang.

"It's Jake," I told Grace as I handed my bill and my money to her, and then I ducked outside.

"Hey," I said.

"Hey yourself. Well, I made it."

"Is it beautiful?" I asked.

"Suzanne, I just left the terminal and I'm standing out here waiting for a squad car to take me into Anchorage, but yeah, it's all pretty breathtaking. Flying in was really something."

"What's the temperature like?"

I could hear the hint of a shiver in his voice. "Colder than I like," he said. "This winter is going to be brutal. I can tell already."

"You'll have to get some long underwear," I said.

"I'm going to need more than that. Oops, it appears that my ride is here. I'll check in later. Love you," Jake said quickly, and then he hung up.

I just laughed as I pocketed my phone.

Grace came out waving my change in the air as she asked, "What's so funny?"

"Jake said it's already freezing up there."

"Literally?" Grace asked incredulously.

"No, of course not. But he did say that it was chilly. I bet it's quite a shock to his North Carolina sensitivities."

"That poor boy," Grace said as she handed me my change.

"Boy? He's a grown man, and a state police instigator at that," I said.

"Maybe so, but he's still a Southern boy at heart."

"I can't disagree with that," I said. "Are you ready to tackle Reggie Nance?"

"I'm more than ready," she said. "Any idea how we can get him to break down and really talk to us about what happened to Jude?"

"There's only one approach that I can think of, and it's pretty risky," I said.

"Go on. Tell me. At least let me judge for myself."

"The only thing that might work, and I want to stress the word might, is we have to invoke Debbie's memory. If we can get him talking about her as sympathetically as we can, he might just spill something that he doesn't want us to know."

Grace frowned.

"What's wrong?"

"Didn't you give *me* a lecture on ethics not that long ago? How is this any better than what I did?"

"It might not be, but we're running out of time, and options," I said. "Do you forgive me if I'm being a little inconsistent about our investigation?"

"Forgiven and forgotten," she said.

"That's why I'm your number one fan," I said.

"As far as you know, anyway," Grace said with a laugh. "Come on, Sherlock. Let's get sleuthing."

Chapter 18

"Reggie, we know you're in there," I said as knocked on his door again. I'd been knocking for three minutes, but so far, he hadn't been interested in answering.

"Suzanne, it appears that he doesn't want to talk to us," Grace said. "Can you imagine that?"

"I guess some folks don't find us as charming as we'd like them to," I answered.

"I don't understand it myself."

"Enough already. I'm here," Reggie said as he finally opened his front door. "What are you two doing here? I'm done talking about Jude Williams."

"That's not why we're here," I said.

"Why should I believe you?" Reggie asked, still standing in the threshold.

"Okay," I said, "what I should have said was that's not the *only* reason that we're here. Mainly, I'd like to hear more about what happened between him and your daughter."

"You know it, and so does everyone else in town," he said.

"I've heard all of the rumors about how it ended, but I'm not talking about that. What I want to know is how he managed to get so close to her in the first place? That's what I don't understand. From everything I knew about Debbie, she was never one to take up with the bad boys, and Jude was that, if nothing else."

"She thought she could change him, can you imagine that?" Reggie asked as he finally stepped outside and joined us.

I shook my head. "I can tell you that she wasn't the first girl to hope that about a boy she thought was worth saving, and she won't be the last, either."

"Why do women do it, then?" he asked. I was sure he'd asked himself that same question a thousand times since his daughter died. "I just can't make any sense out of it."

"We like to believe that our love is enough to touch their hearts and reform them," Grace said softly.

Reggie looked at her with a new perspective. "It's happened to you, too, hasn't it? I can see it in your eyes."

"More than once," Grace said softly, and I felt my heart go out to her. My best friend had experienced one long bad run when it came to the men in her life, and no one knew her pain more than I did.

"Once, maybe I can understand, but what made you do it again, even suspecting how it was all going to end?" Reggie asked as emotion swept over him.

"Where there's life, there is hope, I guess. I truly am sorry about your daughter."

"I appreciate that," he said. "All I ever wanted for her was justice."

"And did you finally get it?" I asked gently.

"I didn't kill him," he said, the edge creeping back into his voice.

"At this moment, I don't care if you did or you didn't," I said. "All I'm asking is now that he's gone, does it ease your pain even in the slightest?"

He looked as though he wanted to cry. "I wish that I could say that it did, but I can't. No, I'm just as empty and dead inside as if the man was still walking around today. I guess the only comfort I'll ever find won't be in this lifetime."

What a sad way to feel. "We need to find out who killed him, Reggie," I said.

"Why?"

It was a fair question. "I'd like to say because his aunt Gabby asked us to, but we were already going to dig into it before she asked us for our help. I suppose it's because what happened to Jude has hung a low cloud over my good friend's wedding, and she deserves better."

"Even though she's marrying your ex-husband?" Reggie asked.

"Even then," I said.

"Well, I'm sorry I can't help you, but I've got nothing to left to say."

He started to walk back into his house, and I could see that Grace was about to say something else, but I shook my head, and she ended up keeping it to herself.

"Why did you stop me?" she asked after Reggie was gone.

"The man's been through enough," I said.

"So then we're just going to give him a free pass?" Grace asked.

"No, but I don't have the heart to beat him up anymore today. Is that okay with you?"

"It's fine," she said as she touched my shoulder lightly. "Are you okay?"

"I'm good," I said, though in truth I was feeling a few different kinds of pain myself at the moment. "Do you feel like tackling Frank Grambling now?"

"We might as well," she said. As we got into my Jeep, Grace asked, "Suzanne, this feels hopeless. How are we *ever* going to solve this case before the wedding?"

"I admit that it's not looking all that promising right now, but you know how these investigations go sometimes. We have to have a lot of different conversations before we hear something that leads us to the truth."

"And we haven't heard anything yet," she said.

"Not that we know of. Maybe Frank will lead us down another path."

"Or maybe he'll be just another dead end," Grace said softly.

"Maybe so, but if he is, we'll just keep digging. It's what we do, remember?"

"Right now, that's pretty hard to forget," she said.

We had just pulled up in front of Frank and Lisa Grambling's house when Grace's cellphone rang. She checked the caller ID and she said, "I've got to take this. It might be a while, Suzanne. Do you want to drive around the block a few times while I talk to my boss?"

"No, you go ahead and take care of business. I'll handle Frank by myself."

"Are you sure you don't need me by your side?" she asked.

"I'll be fine. Besides, you'll be within shouting range if I need you."

"Okay," she said, and then she turned to her cellphone. "Hello. No, that's fine. I can talk."

I left her deep in conversation with her boss as I walked up to the house. That was one thing I didn't have to worry about running the donut shop. I was the boss at Donut Hearts, and no one else could ever tell me what to do. That was the upside, and the downside, too. As the owner and boss, everything ended up on my doorstep, success and failure alike. There was no one else, and in the end, that was the way I preferred it.

I was happy to see that Frank answered the door himself. "Do you have a second?" I asked him.

"What about? My wife's at the grocery store, and I don't want any donuts."

"That works out just fine, because I don't have any," I said.

"Then why are you here?"

"Jude Williams," I said. "I understand that he sold you some fake gold."

"What business is that of yours?" he asked as he stepped outside, getting closer to me than I really would have liked.

"We're trying to find his killer," I said, taking half a step back.

"And you think that's me?" he asked as he stepped

even closer. I could smell the onions on his warm breath, and more than a hint of bourbon. "I'm going to tell you this one more time, and then I'm going to do something. If you don't leave me and my wife alone, you're going to be sorrier than you ever could imagine."

"Is that a threat?" I asked as I decided to stand my ground. I wasn't about to let him bully me if I could help it.

"It sure is," he said, and he took a thick forefinger and pushed me. Ordinarily it wouldn't have been enough to bother me, but he'd caught me off guard, and I stumbled backwards a little.

"Don't you dare touch me," I said, feeling the heat rise in my cheeks.

"Then stay away from me and my family," he said, "or I'll do a lot worse than shove you. You don't want to see that, Suzanne."

He was back inside before I could manage a reply. Having his hand on me, even just his finger, had been unsettling to me, and I felt violated. Bullies pushed. I knew that, but I didn't have to like it. If Frank Grambling had been the one who'd killed Jude Williams, I was going to make sure that he paid for it.

Grace was just hanging up as I came back to the Jeep. After she said her good-byes, she asked me, "Finished already?"

There must have been something in my face that made her alarmed. "Suzanne, what happened?"

"You didn't see it?" I asked.

"No, I was busy talking. Sorry. What did he do?"

"It was nothing," I said, trying to convince myself that it was true.

"Don't lie to me," Grace answered severely.

"He pushed me, okay? It wasn't a big shove; just enough to let me know that he could do a whole lot more damage if he put his mind to it. It shook me up a little, I won't lie to you." Almost as an afterthought, I added, "He threatened me, too; us, as a matter of fact. He said if we don't stop grilling him and his wife, he was going to make us both sorry."

Grace started to get out of the Jeep when I grabbed her arm. "Where do you think you're going?"

"He's not going to get away with that," she said. "At least not if you let go of my arm."

"Grace, it's nothing, and besides, it's already over. Let's just get out of here, okay?"

"Are you sure?"

"I am," I said as I started the Jeep and pulled out. The man was a brute, there was no doubt about that, but that didn't necessarily make him a murderer.

It didn't make him innocent, either. I was going to have to keep my eye on Frank Grambling in the future, and that meant not being alone with him if I could help it. He made me nervous. I couldn't imagine how Lisa felt around him.

"Where are you going now?" Grace asked me as I sped off.

"I thought we might go look for Lisa," I said.

"After what just happened with her husband? Have you lost your mind?"

"I'm not letting someone scare me away from our investigation," I said. "But if you want out, say the word and I won't hold it against you."

"I'm not going anywhere," she said.

"Are you sure?"

"As sure as I've ever been of anything in my life," she replied, and there was no doubting the truth of what she was saying.

"Good. Then let's see if we can track Lisa down."

"Where should we look?" she asked.

"Oh, I forgot to tell you. Frank said that she was at the grocery store."

"Then let's head over there," Grace said.

As it turned out, we got there just in time. Lisa had already finished her shopping, and she was loading her bags into the car.

I pulled up across from her and got out of the Jeep with Grace close on my heels.

"Need a hand with those?" I asked as we walked up to her.

"No, I'm fine," she said absently, and then she realized that it was us. "What are you two doing here? Are you stalking me?"

"We were just doing a bit of shopping ourselves," Grace said before I could answer. It was the right thing to say for two reasons. It might just let us catch her off guard, and it would be hard for Frank to know exactly when we spoke with his wife.

"Then go shop," she said as she threw the last few bags in haphazardly. "I don't have time to talk."

I wouldn't let it go at that, though. "Lisa, did someone get to you?"

"I don't know what you're talking about," she said defiantly.

"The first time we spoke to you, you couldn't tell us fast enough about the people who might want to hurt Jude. The second time we chatted, you practically ran away from us. Something happened between the two times we chatted. You claim that you have a happy life with your husband, so if he didn't threaten you, then who did?"

She looked as though she wanted to tell us; I could see it in her eyes. "I don't know if I can trust you," she finally said.

"We won't tell a soul what you share with us," Grace said in a reassuring voice. "You can bank on it."

"I wish I could," she said. After a long moment, Lisa stared straight into my eyes. "Suzanne, if you or Grace say a word about what I'm about to tell you, I'm a dead woman."

Finally we were breaking through. "You have our words," I said.

Lisa looked up and down the parking lot to see if anyone was near, and then she said, "This could be the end of me, but I can't keep living like this." As she finished, her cellphone rang.

"Let it go to voicemail," Grace said.

"I can't." She answered the call, and her face went pale. "I understand," she said at last then hung up.

"Go on, you were saying?" I asked.

"I can't," she said. Short of blocking her car with our bodies, we couldn't stop her. Lisa raced out of the parking lot, her tires screaming on the pavement.

"Who just called her, Grace?" I asked.

"It had to be her husband," she said.

"Not necessarily. If whoever is threatening her saw her chatting with us just now, it could have been a reminder about what might happen to her." As I said it, I looked wildly around the parking lot for some sign that someone was watching us. There were a few people loading groceries and a few others heading inside, but I didn't see a soul who was directly involved in our investigation. "It's no use. I'm afraid that we might never know."

"Is Lisa in danger?" Grace asked. "Maybe we should follow her."

"We could, but what's the killer going to think if they see us tailing her home? We could put her in more jeopardy than she's already in."

"We need to find out who she's so afraid of," Grace said.

"I don't know how we're going to do that. We can't exactly get her phone records, and we don't have any proof that we can take to Chief Martin to get him to do it, either."

"Well, we have to figure out *some* way to do it," Grace

said.

"I'm trying, but I don't have much hope." My cellphone rang just then, and I found myself hoping that it was Jake again.

It wasn't, and the person on the other end of the line was not someone I wanted to have a conversation with at the moment.

But I didn't really have any choice, so I went ahead and answered anyway.

Chapter 19

"Hello, Gabby," I said. "Listen, I would have called you sooner, but I don't have anything new to report. Grace and I are doing the best that we can, but it hasn't been easy."

"I'm not calling to chide you about not checking in," she said in that particularly disdainful voice she had. "I need you to come to my shop right now."

"We're tracking down clues at the moment," I said. The last thing I wanted was an audience with her.

"You are in the grocery store parking lot, at least you were two minutes ago when I drove past," she said. "This can't wait, Suzanne. Bring Grace with you."

Before I could say another word, she hung up on me.

"What was that all about?" Grace asked me.

"We've been summoned by her highness to ReNEWed," I said.

"We're both about to get scolded, no doubt," Grace said with the hint of a frown. "Doesn't she know we're doing everything we can?"

"I told her that, but it didn't seem to satisfy her."

"I'm shocked," Grace said sarcastically, clearly not surprised by Gabby's attitude at all.

"Nevertheless, we need to go over there," I replied as I headed back to the Jeep.

Grace followed. "Why do I feel like I'm in school and the principal wants to see me?"

"I have the exact same feeling, but we might as well get it over with. If we don't, she'll just keep calling, and worse yet, she'll be even more disapproving."

"I wouldn't wish that on anyone," Grace said. "At least she wants to speak with both of us."

When we got to Gabby's gently used clothing shop, I

saw that the CLOSED sign was in the window and the blinds had been pulled, even though we were in the middle of Gabby's regular work day.

Grace studied the sign and the window treatments. "Are we even sure that she's in there?"

"There's only one way to find out," I said as I knocked firmly on the front door.

"We're closed," I heard a muffled voice say from inside.

"It's Suzanne and Grace," I answered loudly.

"Why didn't you say so?" Gabby asked as she unlocked the door and let us inside.

As we walked across the threshold, I asked her, "Why are you closed in the middle of the afternoon?"

"Soon, it's not going to matter one way or the other, so why bother keeping up pretenses now?" I studied Gabby, and she looked as though she hadn't slept since the last time we'd spoken. Dark circles were under her eyes, and her complexion looked positively waxy.

"Are you okay?" I asked her.

"My last living kin was murdered, and the police think I might have done it," Gabby said. "How do you think I am?"

"Has Chief Martin accused you of anything so far?" I asked her gently. I knew that she was lashing out at me because she was in pain, so I decided to ignore it.

"He comes around here every day with more questions," Gabby said, rubbing her hands together constantly. "If he didn't think I had something to do with it, why won't he leave me alone?"

"He's just doing his job," Grace said.

Gabby wheeled on her. "Is it his job to harass me so much that I can't even sleep at night? Is it his job to ask folks I know around town about me? He's making my life a living nightmare," she said.

"He's just trying to find the truth," I said, trying to speak in a soothing voice. "Gabby, you told me that you didn't kill Jude, so you don't have anything to worry about."

She laughed, but there was no joy in it. "Suzanne, you've been the focus of the chief's investigations before. If this town starts believing that I'm a killer, then I've already been tried and convicted in the only court that really matters."

"I'm sorry, but I don't know what I can do," I said. What she said was true enough. It was too easy to be convicted in the court of public opinion without a shred of solid proof. "If you want me to talk to the chief for you, I will, but I'm not sure that I'd be able to do any good."

"If I wanted someone with influence over the man to intervene for me, I would have called your mother, Suzanne."

I didn't like that implication, but again, I let it slide. "Gabby, you called us, remember?" I asked. "If we're here talking to you, we can't track down Jude's real killer."

"I wanted you to be the first to know about my decision," Gabby said, softening for just a moment. "We have been friends for a long time, so I thought it only right to tell you first."

"What's going on?"

"I just wanted you to know that if you two *or* the police fail to find the killer in the next twenty-four hours, I'm shutting this place down and starting over somewhere else," she said. "I'm selling the business, and my house as well. I just can't stand living under this cloud of suspicion, and if it doesn't go away quickly, I'm not going to have any choice."

"Gabby, you don't mean that," I said.

"But I do," she answered as she looked fondly around her shop. "This has been a good life, but I won't stay if I feel as though the folks in April Springs are constantly whispering behind my back. I've given my life to this place. It makes me so sad that instead of being there for my nephew, I was here sending out e-mails to customers I thought might like what I had to offer."

"Hang on a second," I said. "You were *working* while you were here?"

"Yes, I had to do something, didn't I? Why does it matter?"

"Let me see your computer," I said.

"What's going on, Suzanne?" Grace asked.

"Hang on. Let me check something first."

Gabby led us in back to her office and showed us her computer. "What good is this going to do?"

"You said that you e-mailed customers that night," I said. "Did any of them respond to you?"

"Suzanne, I have very selective clients. They know that if they want something I'm offering, they have to respond quickly, or it will be gone. Of course I chatted online with several of them, but no one actually saw me here."

"Maybe they didn't have to," I said. "Call up your account, and go to the Sent Messages file."

She looked unsure of where I was going with it, but Grace got it instantly. She winked at me and smiled, but we weren't out of the woods yet.

"Here you go," she said after a few moments.

"May I?" I asked.

"Go right ahead. I don't have anything to hide from you."

I studied her e-mails, taking particular care to look at the time of each of them. After a minute, I looked at Gabby and said, "I'm calling the chief."

"Why?" Gabby asked. "Did I do something wrong?"

"On the contrary. You were here chatting with customers during Jude's time of death. You're in the clear, Gabby."

"Is it really that simple?" she asked, clearly not believing me.

"Once the chief confirms that the folks you chatted with vouch for you, I can't see a problem with your alibi. Gabby, working may have just saved you."

"Then what are you waiting for? Call him, Suzanne."

I called the chief and explained my theory to him.

"I'll send someone over to verify all of this," the chief said. "In the meantime, nobody should touch that computer."

"Absolutely," I said. "We'll all be here."

He added softly, "That's good work, Suzanne. I didn't even think to ask about e-mailing after she told me that she was alone and that she didn't see anyone the entire time."

"Don't give me too much credit. I just picked up on it during a casual conversation."

"Still, it was a nice catch. Jake would be proud."

I felt a twinge at that, but I swallowed it quickly. "Thanks."

"What did he say?" Gabby asked me as soon as I hung up.

"One of his people is on their way. We're not supposed to touch anything in the meantime."

Grace promptly reached out and touched the computer monitor. "Call me a rebel," she said.

"I'll call you whatever you want me to," Gabby said as a smile came tentatively forward. "I don't know how to thank you two enough."

"Thank her," Grace said as she pointed to me. "Suzanne is the real sleuth in the outfit."

"You're a team," Gabby said, "and I'm thanking you both."

"We're just happy to help," I said. "So, does this change your plans in any way?"

"I'm staying," she said, and then she added, "What am I doing staying closed? I have to open the shop back up. I'm sure you two have somewhere else you need to be."

"Don't you want us to wait with you for the police?" I

asked her.

"I can take things from here," Gabby said as she walked us to the front. "You two have work to do. Just because you proved that I wasn't the killer doesn't mean that the real murderer is going to get caught without more work on your parts. Now shoo."

As we walked out front, Gabby opened the blinds and flipped her sign over. Out on the sidewalk, Grace looked at me and said, "It's your fault, you know."

"What's my fault?" I asked.

"Gabby was ready to leave town forever, and you just single-handedly gave her a reason to stay. Way to go, Suzanne."

I grinned at my best friend. "I don't even care. Let her stay. She has as much right to be here as anyone else."

"I'm going to remind you that you said that the next time she gets on your nerves," Grace said.

"Go right ahead." Gabby and I had experienced our differences in the past, but all in all, it was a comfort having her nearby. So much was changing in my world in April Springs that it was nice having something that I could count on. Warts and all, Gabby was one of those things that I relied on to make sure that my world would continue to spin long after all of the births, weddings, and funerals.

"Now it's time to focus on the last three suspects we *haven't* spoken with today," I told Grace once we were back in my Jeep. "I'm not really excited about doing it, but we really don't have any choice."

"Are we really going to talk to Emily again?" she asked me. "Suzanne, she's not exactly your biggest fan right now, is she?"

"It can't be helped," I said, even though I agreed with Grace completely. "If it's all the same to you, though, I'd rather tackle Peter and Max again first."

"I can't blame you for leaving Emily for last," Grace said as we drove toward Max's place.

"Listen, if you want to hang back when I speak with Emily, I understand. There's no sense in *both* of us getting banned from attending the wedding."

Grace looked at me with a surprised expression on her face. "Suzanne, were you really under the impression that I would go *without* you?"

"I just assumed that you would," I said.

"Well, you were wrong. Sure, I'll get them a nice present, but if you're not going, then neither am I."

"But you're in the wedding," I protested.

"The second I learned that Emily dropped you, I bowed out. She didn't like it, but she understood. Suzanne, you and I have been friends for a lot longer than Emily and I have been."

"You didn't have to do that for me," I said.

"Oh, but I did." Grace shrugged, and then she asked, "Now, how are we going to approach Max and Peter? Should we split them up, or grill them together?"

"I'm just hoping that we find them at Max's place," I said. "I haven't thought it through beyond that, to be honest with you."

Grace grinned. "Even better. We'll play it by ear. I believe our investigations always go better when we fly by the seats of our pants, don't you?"

"It appears to be the best way we know how to investigate," I replied with a grin.

"Max, we need to talk," I said as he answered the door.

My ex-husband replied with the hint of a smile despite our earlier differences, "Boy, in the old days, that would have sent chills down my spine."

"But no more?"

"No more," he said, almost laughing as he spoke.

"Why are you in such a good mood all of a sudden?" I

asked him. It wasn't *entirely* uncharacteristic, but it did strike me as odd, given the cloud of the murder hovering over his impending wedding day.

"I'm getting married tomorrow," he said. "And if that itself isn't reason enough to be happy, I just got a call from Victor White. You know Vic, don't you?"

Vic White was a heavyset man with a penchant for raspberry-filled donuts, and not a week went by when he didn't come by to pick up a dozen or two. "Of course I know him; he's the main reason I have to keep reordering raspberry filling."

"Well, I'm so happy that I could kiss his bearded face right now," Max said.

"This I've got to hear. And thanks for that image, by the way. It's going to take me days to get that out of my head."

"You're welcome."

"So, why are you so happy to hear from Vic?" Grace asked. "Does he owe you money?"

"It's even better than that. He just got back into town, and he wants to try out for Falstaff in my latest production." When Max wasn't acting, he was directing our own local community theater.

"I thought you just used older actors," I said. Max was notorious for mining all of his talent from the Senior Center.

"Sometimes I cast outside of my core group," he said. "Anyway, Vic left town the night Jude was murdered, and he just now got back. I'm the one who told him the news about what happened."

"I'm still waiting to hear why that makes you so happy," I said.

"Vic saw Jude downtown alone by the clock an *hour* after Emily and Jude had their little chat. It proves that he was still alive after they spoke. That's got to go a long way toward clearing her, don't you think?"

"You might be right," I said.

"I know that I am. I was about to call the police chief when you rang my doorbell. My bride is about to be cleared of all suspicion," Max said.

I didn't know that I'd go that far, but it did look better for Emily than it had yet. In order for her to have killed him, she would have had to track Jude down again an hour after they spoke. "It still doesn't prove that she's innocent," I said.

"As a matter of fact, it does. You see, given the new potential times of death, Emily has her own mother as an alibi, along with three of her cousins. They were all working on the wedding together."

"That *is* good news," I said. "Be sure to tell her that I'm happy it worked out that way."

"But don't you see?" Max asked as he hugged me. "That means that you're back in the wedding."

"Not so fast," I said. "That's Emily's call, but even if she invited me now, there may be too much bad blood between us to make a difference. No, I believe that I'll skip the festivities, if it's all the same to you."

Max's smile faded. "You don't mean that, Suzanne."

"Is it really *that* important to you that I come to your wedding?"

"There wouldn't even be a wedding without you," Max said.

"I'm sure you two would have worked things out on your own," I said. "Don't give me too much credit; I don't deserve it."

"You're selling yourself too short," Max said, and then he turned to Grace. "Talk some sense into her, would you? You two can come together."

"Sorry, but I've already bailed out, too," Grace said.

"What is it with you both? Can't you just be happy for me?" He looked genuinely distraught now.

"We're happy for you," I said. "Right, Grace?"

"Absolutely. We're just not coming."

"Fine. Whatever," Max said. "Nothing's going to get

me down today. I'm getting married tomorrow."

"In spite of the murder investigation?" Grace asked him.

"Why should that matter now? As soon as I tell Chief Martin what Vic told me, Emily is off the hook."

"I hate to bring this up," I said, "but you and Peter have to still be on his list."

"None of that matters," Max said. "I know that we're innocent, and that's all that counts."

"I'm not sure the chief is going to feel the same way," I said as my cellphone rang. It was Chief Martin himself. "Speak of the devil and he appears," I said.

"If that's the chief, I want to talk to him," Max said.

"Let me see what he wants first," I answered as I stepped away to take the call.

"What's going on, Chief?" I asked.

"Good news, at least for your ex and his best man," the chief said.

"I'm listening," I replied, not wanting to give anything away.

"One of my officers was interviewing folks who had rooms near the one where the two of them were the night of the murder, and she hit pay dirt."

"What did she find?"

"It's kind of sad, really. A man in the room next to theirs was out on the balcony the entire time Max and Peter were there. He can alibi both of them."

That seemed like a piece of good luck for Max and Peter. "He never left for one minute?"

"The man was thinking about jumping, if you can believe that, but he heard voices, so while he was waiting for them to go back inside, he sat there in the dark and listened. Evidently Max was so enthusiastic about living that he actually convinced the man not to jump after all."

"He's going to love hearing that. I'll let you tell him yourself, since he's right here."

"Suzanne, I don't mind if you pass on the news yourself," the chief said.

"Actually, he has a bit of news himself he wants to share."

After a moment's pause, the chief said, "Put him on, then."

"The chief wants to speak with you," I said as I handed Max my cellphone.

"What was that all about?" Grace asked me softly as Max relayed the same story to Chief Martin that he had to us.

"Max and Peter are in the clear. A witness was next door on his balcony, and he eavesdropped on them both the entire time they were there, so neither man could have killed Jude."

"Wow, what are the odds of that?"

"It's lucky it happened," I said, "but it was good police work uncovering it. The chief is a lot better at his job than most folks give him credit for."

"Including you?" Grace asked with a smile.

"What do you mean?"

"You haven't always been his biggest fan, especially since he started dating your mother."

"A person's entitled to change her opinion, isn't she?" I asked.

"Absolutely. You're living proof of that. If I'd told you right after your divorce that you'd ever end up being friendly with Max again, you would have laughed in my face."

"So, maybe I'm not the only one with the capacity to change," I said as Max hung up and handed my cellphone back to me. "What did he say?"

"He's headed over to Vic's right now," Max said happily.

"Did he tell you the other news?" I asked.

"About our friendly neighbor hiding in the shadows? He did," Max said, his smile broader still. "It was lucky for us, wasn't it?"

"It sounds as though you had a hand in keeping that man from jumping," I said.

Max, never one to decline credit in the past, just shook his head. "I don't know if I'd say that."

"You don't have to," I said. "The chief told me as much himself."

"Then it was a lucky night for all three of us," Max said. "I can't wait to tell Emily. There's nothing stopping us from getting married now."

After we left him, Grace said, "It's funny how things work out sometimes."

"It is," I agreed. "We're closing in now. I can feel it."

"Unless we don't even know the real killer," she said.

"I suppose it's possible, but my gut is telling me that it's one of our remaining three suspects."

"Then even though Max, Peter, and Emily might be out of this, we've still got a lot of work to do, don't we?" Grace asked.

"We do," I agreed.

"What do we do now?"

"Honestly, I don't have a clue," I said.

Chapter 20

We were heading back into town when my cellphone rang again.

"Hi, Momma." I had to hide the disappointment in my voice when I answered my mother's call, since I'd been hoping that it was Jake. Clearly he couldn't call me every half hour with updates. I knew that it was an unreasonable expectation, but that didn't make it any easier to take. "What's going on?"

"You're eating at home tonight, aren't you?"

"That depends," I said with a smile. "What are we having?"

She laughed. "Oh, no, you're not about to catch me in that particular trap. I've been cooking all afternoon, so is there really any doubt in your mind if it's any good or not?"

"No, ma'am," I replied. "I withdraw the question."

There was a pause on the other end, and then Momma asked, "Is something wrong?"

The woman could read me as easily as she could large print. "Actually, we've gotten some good news, but Grace and I are still having trouble figuring out how to catch Jude Williams' killer."

"You can tell me all about it over dinner," Momma said. "Bring Grace. Goodness knows that I made plenty."

"Will the police chief be joining us?" I asked.

"No, Phillip is eating at his desk these days," she said. "I may take a plate to him later."

I did my best not to laugh. Momma had done that more and more as the chief had worked late. I had to give the man credit. When he'd first started trying to woo my mother, he'd hit a solid wall of resistance, but he'd been determined, and now she was bringing him food to his office. "That's nice."

She must have heard a hint of humor in my voice, despite my best efforts to hide it. "That's enough of that, young lady."

"Yes, ma'am," I said. "Grace and I will be there."

"Good. I'm looking forward to it."

After we hung up, Grace asked, "Did I just accept a dinner invitation without knowing it?"

"You did," I said. "Is that okay?"

"It's fantastic," Grace said, "as long as your mother's cooking."

"Hey, I'm a good cook, too," I said.

"As good as your mother?"

I just shook my head. There was no doubt in anyone's mind who the superior chef was in my family. Grace tapped my arm as I drove home. When I turned toward her, she said, "Suzanne, *nobody* makes a donut as good as you do."

"You know what? I'll take it."

"You should. Did she tell you what we're having?"

"It's going to be a surprise, I guess," I said.

"Ordinarily I'm not a big fan of surprises, but in this case, I'll make an exception," Grace replied with a smile. She was as fond of my mother's cooking as I was.

"Wow, that smells amazing," I told Momma as Grace and I walked into the kitchen. "I love your lasagna."

"That's good, because, as usual, I made much too much," she said as she smiled at the comment. My mother was an excellent cook, but she was so much more than that. She was a shrewd businesswoman who owned properties and businesses *I* didn't even know about. To say that she kept her financial affairs secret would be the understatement of the century. Given how much she was probably worth, it still amazed me that we still lived in our charming little cottage on the edge of April Springs' park. The cottage had sentimental value to both of us, though. Built by our family long ago, it was where she had lived with my father and me, and that made it priceless in both our points of view.

"You can never make too much lasagna," Grace said with a twinkle in her eye.

"I'm glad you feel that way, because I'm sending some home with you tonight."

"You don't have to twist my arm," Grace said.

"There'll still be enough for us to have leftovers though, right?" I asked.

Momma patted my shoulder. "Never fear, Suzanne. Our freezer is full as it is."

"But not with lasagna," I said. "Did you make cheddar-chive loaf, too?" I asked as I spotted the dark brown loaves on the cooling rack. Momma had taken a basic recipe and modified it to yield the most savory bread imaginable, filled with sharp cheddar cheese, fresh green scallions, and just the right amount of thyme and other spices. It was great fresh out of the oven with butter melting into the crevasses of the bread, but it was at its best after it had cooled and was toasted, at least in my opinion.

"I made it this morning," Momma said. "I'll toast a batch of it as soon as the lasagna is nearly ready."

"Is there anything that we can do?" Grace asked.

"Thanks, but I've got it covered. We've got twenty minutes before the lasagna is ready, so if you two would like to sit out on the porch and enjoy this glorious weather we're having, that's fine by me."

"Thanks, Momma," I said as I kissed her cheek. Grace buzzed the other one, and Momma smiled.

"Off with you now," she said playfully, and Grace and I took her advice and retreated to the porch.

"We are going to feast like royalty tonight," Grace said once she was situated on the porch swing.

"We do most nights around here," I admitted as I grabbed one of the rocking chairs. That was what I loved about our porch. It was wide enough to hold a party on and always offered protection from the elements. As a child, I could remember curling up on the swing wrapped in a blanket and watching it snow.

"So, what's our plan of attack with our remaining suspects?" Grace asked me.

"We can't just keep questioning them and hope that somebody breaks," I said after some thought. "That's not going to work anymore."

"What else did you have in mind?"

"Grace, you know I hate to do it because it can be scary-dangerous, but I don't think we have any other options left. We have to set a trap for our killer."

Grace took that in, and then she asked, "I can see your point, but what are we going to use as bait?"

"That's the question, isn't it? I don't really want to use anybody else if we can help it. It's not fair to ask someone else to assume a risk that we're not willing to take ourselves."

Grace breathed heavily, and then said, "Okay. I'll do it."

"We both will," I said. "I just wish that Jake was here to back us up. It's not going to do us any good if we trap the killer and they turn the tables on us."

"We can't exactly ask the police for help," Grace said.

"No, my relationship with the Chief Martin is good, but it's not that good. If he finds out what we're planning to do, he'll shut us down in a heartbeat. There's only one option as far as I can see."

As I reached for my cellphone, Grace asked, "Who are you going to call?"

"I think it would be neighborly if we invited the mayor over for dinner, don't you? You heard Momma. She made more than she knows what to do with, and besides, she likes George."

"Are we really going to drag him into this?" Grace asked me.

"Drag? Are you kidding? He's been dying to get involved again. Besides, we really don't have any other options left."

"I wouldn't mention that particular fact to him when he comes," Grace said.

"I wasn't planning to," I said as I dialed the mayor's number.

"George, what are your dinner plans tonight?" I asked as he answered my call.

"I thought I'd drift over to the Boxcar a little later," he said. "Make me a better offer, and I'm there."

"Don't you like Trish's cooking anymore?" I asked playfully.

"I love it, but it does tend to run to type, doesn't it? I'd just about kill for a homemade meal."

"Well, homicide isn't on the menu, but Momma just made lasagna, and you're welcome to join us. Can you make it in twenty minutes?"

"I'll be there in two," he said as he hung up.

I stood. "I'll be right back."

"Where are you going?"

"To tell Momma that we're having more company."

I made it back to the front porch fast enough, but George was already there. "What did you do, strap on a jetpack and *fly* over here?" I asked.

"I was in the neighborhood," he said. "Thanks for the invitation."

"You're most welcome. Momma was delighted to hear that you'd be joining us."

George started to stand. "You didn't ask her first? Suzanne, I can't stay under those circumstances."

"Sit back down, your honor," I said with a grin. "This isn't entirely a neighborly invitation. Grace and I need your help in our investigation."

The mayor sat back down with a broad smile on his face. "All I can say is that it's about time. Now tell me, who are we going to go after?"

"There are three of them, as a matter of fact," I said.

"It's going to be a trap, is it?" George asked. "I'm happy to be the bait."

"Actually, we were hoping that you could be our enforcer. Once the trap is sprung, we need you to be there to keep us from ending up like Jude Williams."

"I can do that," George said with a frown.

"Is there something wrong?" I asked.

"I'd rather be the one in danger, truth be told," he said.

I patted his arm. "We appreciate that, but it won't work that way. The killer has to think that Grace and I have information about him or her that we're going to turn over to the police. Since you haven't been involved in the case all along, they won't buy that you've got it." I paused, and then I added, "If you're not comfortable doing it, we can ask someone else. We just thought you'd like to be involved." He was honestly our last option, but I didn't want to let him know that.

"No, that's fine. I'll do it. When are we going to spring this trap?" he asked eagerly.

"We haven't decided yet," I said.

"Well, if you want my opinion, the sooner the better," George said. "If we wait too long, we could end up missing out altogether."

"My, you're eager to get started, aren't you?" Grace asked him lightly.

"Yes, but I've got another motivation as well," the mayor said. "Polly's coming back home tomorrow, and I'm not sure that she'd approve of me being your muscle. If we could manage it tonight, that would be great."

"It's short notice, but I think we can do it," I said. "What do you say, Grace?"

"It's not a bad idea. How exactly are we going to set the trap?"

After a few moments of thought, I said, "How about

this? We tell all three suspects that a witness is coming by the donut shop at five AM with some critical new information, and then we wait. I'll send Emma home early on some pretext after we finish the donuts. Grace, George, if you both want to be in this, I'm afraid that you're going to have to get up pretty early."

"It's not a problem for me," the mayor said. "I'm usually up around four anyway."

"Really?" Grace asked him incredulously.

"The older I get, the less sleep I seem to need," George said.

"Well, it's going to be a sacrifice for me, but I'll manage somehow," Grace said.

"Good. Now all that's left is contacting our suspects," I said, just as Momma came out onto the porch.

"Contacting them about what?" she asked.

"It's not important," I said, hoping that Momma would let it slide.

To my delight, she did. As she extended a hand to George, she said, "So lovely to have you, Mr. Mayor."

"Thank you," George said. "Sorry to be sprung on you at the last second."

"Nonsense. I should have thought of it myself. If you are all ready, dinner is served."

After a lovely meal, Momma said, "I hate to dash off, but I promised Phillip a plate tonight."

"Go. We'd be delighted to do the dishes," Grace said.

"It's the least we can do," I added.

"And I'll supervise to make sure the job's done right," George finished as he winked at my mother. The mayor was certainly in a good mood, no doubt because he was back on our investigative team, albeit briefly.

"I trust that you'll watch out for my girls," Momma said to him in a serious manner.

"I'll guard them with my life," he said in all earnestness.

"I know you will," she said as she patted his cheek. "I'm sure you know that if anything were to happen to them, there is no describing the level of my wrath."

"I'm well aware of it," George said.

Momma smiled brightly. "Then I'm off."

After she was gone, I told George, "She knows what we're up to."

"She called me one of her girls," Grace said proudly.

"Of course you are," George said. "And Suzanne, your mother is a brilliant woman. I'm sure it wasn't that tough figuring out what we were up to."

"Then let's get these dishes done and get started," I said. "We have a busy night ahead of us."

As we washed and dried the dishes, we finalized our plans.

"Okay, here's the finished plan," I said. "Tell me if either one of you spot any flaws in it. Grace, you and I are going to visit each suspect—in one case, two in one house—and we're going to apologize for the trouble we've caused in our investigation. Then we're going to drop the bomb that there is an eyewitness who won't talk to the police without us. We don't even know who it is yet; they left me a note at the donut shop. They will be meeting us at the diner at five, and the police are coming at six. We don't know the details yet, but we're in it up to our eyebrows."

"What am I supposed to do while all of this is going on?" George asked.

"You're going to be tailing us to make sure none of our suspects decide to jump the gun. Are you armed right now?"

"I don't usually carry a weapon to dinner," George said.

"Then we'll wait until you can go home and get one," I said. Honestly, I felt better knowing that George would be watching us from the shadows. He'd been a good cop before he'd retired, and I knew that he was a man we could count on. "What do you think? Have I missed anything?"

"It's a simple plan, but it should be effective," George said.

"It sounds good to me, except for the part about us being the cheese in the trap," Grace said.

I took her soapy hands in mine. "Grace, this will work just as well if I'm the only bait we use."

"No, thanks. I'm going to be right there with you, Suzanne. If anything happens to you, it's going to happen to me, too."

George said, "Ladies, while you're under my protection, nothing is going to happen to either *one* of you. I promise you."

"Don't make promises you can't keep," Grace said.

"You don't doubt me, do you?" George asked with a hint of hurt in his voice.

She put a hand on his shoulder. "George, I trust you with my life."

"Good. Then let's finish these dishes so that we can get started," he said.

Chapter 21

Before I rang the doorbell at Lisa and Frank's house, I looked around behind me. There was no sign of our escort. "George, are you there?" I whispered.

"I'm here," he said so softly that I almost missed him.

"Shh. Someone's already coming to the door," Grace said as she tugged on my arm.

I knocked before they could open it, so when they did, it wouldn't appear as though they'd caught us doing something that we shouldn't have been doing.

So I hoped.

Lisa opened the door slightly as she said, "Go away."

"Is your husband at home?" I asked her.

Suspicion quickly crossed her face. "What do you want with Frank?"

"Who's there?" I heard him ask from inside.

"It's nobody," Lisa said.

"It's Suzanne and Grace," I said loud enough to be sure that he heard.

"Now you've done it," Lisa hissed at me.

I wasn't going to let that deter me. "I'm sorry, but I need to speak with both of you."

She was still frowning at us when Frank came into view. The look of anger and disgust on his face was palpable, and I was suddenly glad that we'd brought George with us. "I don't know what it's going to take to get my message across, but words obviously aren't enough." He started to roll up his sleeves as he came toward us, and I heard movement behind us. I had to end this before George was exposed and our plans were blown.

"There's no need to be upset. We came to apologize," I said quickly.

The movement behind us stopped as Frank halted his forward progress. "Go on. We're listening," he said.

"We never should have bothered you in the first place, and we're very sorry about it. Grace and I just wanted to come say that in person."

"We accept your apology," Lisa said quickly as she tried to pull her husband back inside, no doubt so they could slam the door in our faces.

"Not so fast," he said as he jerked his arm free. Turning back to me, he asked, "Why the sudden change of heart, Suzanne?"

That was the question I'd been hoping for. "We actually just got a break in the case."

"What happened?" he asked.

"Someone spotted the killer right after they hit Jude Williams with that iron bar," I said. "They've been afraid to come forward up until now, but they're coming by the donut shop at five tomorrow morning to tell the police everything."

"How does this involve you?"

"Whoever witnessed the murder won't say a word unless we're right there with them," I said.

"So *you* don't even know who it is?" he asked.

"Not yet, but that's going to be resolved soon enough," Grace replied. "We truly are sorry for inconveniencing you with all of our questions."

"You've made your apologies," Lisa said. Was she that afraid? If it wasn't her husband who had spooked her, someone else had done a pretty good job of it. "Thanks for stopping by."

This time Frank allowed himself to be pulled back inside. There was an odd look on his face, as though he was still mulling over what we'd just told him. Neither one of them had done anything overt to make them look guilty, but neither did they act innocent.

Once we were back in the Jeep, I drove down the street and then pulled into a parking space. George soon parked right behind me, and he got out and approached the Jeep.

"That was close," he said. "I thought he was going to come after you, and I wasn't sure that I could get there in time."

"It worked out fine, though, didn't it? That's really all that counts."

"You handled him like a pro, Suzanne," George said. "You didn't even really need me there watching your back."

"Don't kid yourself," Grace said, the relief clear in her voice. "If you hadn't been there, I would have jumped off that porch the second Frank came out."

"I'm just glad that I could finally help," the mayor said, clearly pleased that he'd been able to back us up.

"Two down, and one to go," I said. "Are we ready to tackle Reggie now?"

"Give me a minute to get there ahead of you," George said.

"You've got it."

Before George left to return to his own car, he looked at us and said, "I know I shouldn't say this, but this is kind of fun, isn't it?"

"It's actually pretty dangerous," I said, reminding him that we weren't playing around. We were baiting a killer, and things could still go horribly wrong for us if our plan didn't work.

"I know, but I miss the excitement. It's just not the same presiding over a city council meeting, or sitting in on the zoning board."

"We'll try not to stimulate your level of excitement too much," I said as I fought back a yawn. "If I'm going to get any sleep at all tonight, we need to make this quick."

"Got it, boss," he said, and then he actually trotted back to his car. George had suffered a pretty severe leg injury once upon a time helping me, and it was nice to see that he'd fully recovered from it.

I just hoped no one else got hurt because of one of my investigations. It had nearly made me swear off any amateur sleuthing in the future, but circumstances kept dragging me back in. It appeared that for me, there was no getting away from it.

"Hi, Reggie," I said when he answered the door ten minutes later.

"What are you two doing here?" he asked as he looked at Grace and me. It was pretty clear that he wasn't all that happy about seeing either one of us. It seemed to be the night for it, but I decided not to take it personally.

"We came to apologize," Grace said, beating me to it.

"About?" he asked.

"Everything," I answered. After I repeated our story, I concluded by saying, "We meant no disrespect to you or your daughter. I hope that you can find it in your heart to forgive us."

"We're okay," Reggie said. "Now, if you'll excuse me, I'm watching a movie."

"That's all we wanted to say," I said, and Grace and I left the porch.

George followed us again, and we stopped by the clock near city hall. "That was all relatively painless, wasn't it?" the mayor said. It was clear that he was actually a little disappointed by the lack of action. "What do we do now?"

I didn't even try to hide my yawn this time. "I don't know about you two, but I'm going home to get as much sleep as I can. No matter how this plays out in the end, I still have donuts to make tomorrow."

"How can you do that, knowing that you're going to confront a killer tomorrow?" George asked me.

"How could you put on your uniform and strap your gun on every day when you were a cop, knowing that something very bad could happen to you at any time?" I asked him.

"That was different. It was just all part of the job."

"Well, that's the way it is with me. Rain or shine,

snow or sun, I make donuts. It's what I do, but it's more than that. It's a part of me."

"Can you ever envision yourself doing anything else?" Grace asked me softly.

"I don't honestly know," I said. "Given the right circumstances, I might be able to find another passion in my life."

"Like for someone currently in Alaska?" George asked.

I just laughed. "Good night, George."

"Night, ladies. I'll see you both bright and early."

"I'm counting on it," I said, and then I drove Grace home.

As I pulled up in front of her house, she hesitated before getting out. "Suzanne, do you regret your decision not to go to Alaska with Jake?"

"Do you want to know the truth?" I asked her.

"I wouldn't have asked you otherwise."

"I *still* might end up there," I said after a long moment of silence.

"Are you thinking about joining him?" she asked, clearly surprised by my answer.

"I'm considering it," I said. "Would you ever be able to forgive me if I did?"

She didn't even hesitate. "Suzanne, I would never hold following your heart against you. Just make sure to get a place with enough room for me to visit. I've got vacation saved up, so be warned. If you end up going, I'll be coming your way soon."

"I'm counting on it," I said, "but I haven't made any decisions one way or the other yet."

"In the end, you'll make the right one. I'm sure of it."

"I wish I could be that sure myself. Good night, Grace."

"Good night, Suzanne. I'll see you in a few hours."

"Sorry about that," I said. "If there had been any other way, I would have made the time closer to your liking, say noon."

"Yes, we need to work on that in the future," she said with a smile as she got out.

"Will do," I said, and then I drove the short distance down the road home.

Momma was back already; at least her car was in its spot, and from the way the cottage was lit up, I expected to walk in and see her sitting on her usual spot on the sofa reading her latest mystery.

What I found inside, though, was something entirely, and frighteningly, different.

Chapter 22

"Put the knife down, Lisa," I said in horror as I saw that she held a long blade to my mother's throat. "You don't want to do something that you're going to regret." It appeared that our trap had indeed caught a rat, just too soon for us to react in time.

"I'll put it down when you tell me who your source is, and don't try to feed me that bull that you don't know who it is. You made it pretty clear that you knew, or at least that you thought you did. I'll take whatever name you've got."

"It was all just a ruse," I said, trying to be as transparently truthful as I could be. "We wanted to trap the killer, so we made up that story. We didn't think that you'd react before you found out who the eyewitness really was."

"Why would I do that, when you made it so easy for me to take you out first? By we, I'm assuming you mean you and Grace."

"Who knows? There could be more," I said, hoping to change her mind from killing my mother and me. I turned to look at my mother and I asked, "Are you okay, Momma?"

"I'm fine, dear," she said.

Lisa dug the knife in a little, and a line of blood trickled down Momma's skin. "I told you not to say a word when Suzanne got home," Lisa said angrily.

"My daughter asked me a question," she said.

"I don't care if the Queen of Hearts asks you to tea; the next word you say will be your last, and when I'm finished with you, I'll kill your daughter, too."

Momma didn't respond, but I did see her eyes dart over to the closet where we kept a baseball bat on hand for protection. It wouldn't have done us much good if Lisa had brought a gun, but in a knife fight, it could come in pretty handy.

But I had to get to it without Momma dying first, and that I could not imagine doing.

"Why did you kill Jude?" I asked. "Was it because of the fake gold he sold your husband, or because he was done with you?"

Lisa shook her head. "Don't try to be clever, Suzanne; it doesn't suit you. Who do you think gave Jude that gold-plated junk in the first place? I knew that it was worthless, but I also realized that my husband wouldn't be able to tell. It was supposed to be our seed money."

I nodded as though I understood. "So, no to the gold, but yes on the rejection."

She held the knife closer to my mother's throat when I said that, and I heard Momma gasp. "Really, Suzanne? Do you honestly want to anger the woman with your mother's life in her hands? I'd watch my tone, if I were you."

"But you were clearly afraid of something or someone the last time we spoke," I said. "You were going to tell Grace and me something important when you were interrupted by a phone call."

Lisa smiled, and I felt the hairs on the back of my neck stand up as she said, "It was all just an act. I was afraid that you two knew more than you were letting on. The phone call was a convenient way to stall you until I could find out just how *much* you knew. After all, I didn't want to have to kill you both if I didn't have to. You really shouldn't say anything bad about Jude to me."

This woman had clearly gone off the deep end. I was going to have to find a way to appease her without endangering my mother any more than I already had. "Take it easy, Lisa. I didn't mean anything by what I said about him."

"I know *exactly* what you meant," she said, and then her face softened. "What happened to Jude was an accident, something that couldn't be helped. He was going to leave without me, despite all of our plans. I had to convince him that he needed me."

I never thought that I'd ever hear a killer describe hitting her victim with an iron bar and killing him as an accident.

"Tell the police that," I said, trying to be as convincing as I could. "I'm sure that they'll believe you if you just tell your side of the story."

"They aren't ever going to hear it. After I take care of you two and Grace, I'll be long gone."

"What about Frank?" I asked.

Her grin was chilling. "Nobody's going to check on my dear husband anytime soon. I'm expecting him to bleed out at any minute. At least *that* man deserved what he got."

And there it was. No matter what she said, Lisa was planning to kill everyone.

Not if I could help it.

I started to move, and Momma must have seen something, because she shook her head slightly before I could implement my plan. The knife bit in a little deeper as she did, but her movement served its purpose.

I stopped dead in my tracks.

Instead, Momma said loudly, "We're in here."

"Who are you talking to?" Lisa asked as she loosened her grip on the knife for just one second.

Momma must have been able to feel it, because she grabbed Lisa's knife hand with both of hers and fought to get control of the blade.

She didn't fight alone, though.

"Run, Suzanne," my mother commanded.

I never even gave it a single thought. At that moment, I didn't think about the baseball bat, a gun, or even a tank.

All I could think about was helping my mother.

The blade was turned toward my mother's neck again,

and I could see that she was quickly losing the battle. If I didn't do something, and quickly, she would be slashed with it.

I threw myself straight into the fray, grappling with the knife as Momma and I fought Lisa for control.

She was strong, though, stronger than I bargained for. Was it that edge of craziness that was powering her? Whatever it was, I could see that despite all odds, we were losing the battle. The blade dipped closer and closer, nearer to my mother's precious skin.

I had to make a decision, and I had to do it quickly.

In an instant, I took my hands off the hilt of the blade and went straight for her throat.

She wasn't going to kill my mother, not while I was standing by.

If nothing else, my direct attack made Lisa drop the knife in surprise and claw at my hands for a breath.

I wouldn't let up, though.

She'd just tried to kill my mother, and in my mind, she'd forfeited all rights to my mercy. I felt her hands on mine weaken as I pressed harder and harder, doing my utmost to choke the life out of her.

Suddenly, there was a faint whisper in my ear. "Stop, Suzanne. We've won."

I tried to shake her off, but she told me again in that gentle voice of hers, "Stop."

I finally loosened my grip, and I heard Lisa gasping for breath. "Are you crazy?" she tried to shout. "You could have killed me." Evidently I'd bruised something important in her throat, because it came out in a raspy voice.

"That was the general idea," I said as I stood up and grabbed the knife. "Momma, do we still have that rope in the hall closet?"

"Yes, it's still there," she said, clearly relieved that I'd stopped in time. If she hadn't been there, who knew? Then again, if Lisa hadn't threatened my mother, I never would have tried to choke the life out of her.

"Get it, and tie her up. After that, I need you to give the police chief a call."

"Shouldn't I call him *first*?" Momma asked as she stood there looking down at Lisa.

"No," I ordered. "Get the rope first, and then make the call."

"Yes, dear," she said as though I'd asked her to pass the pepper at the dinner table.

Once I had the rope, I knelt down low to Lisa. "If you move, I'm going to finish what I started. Do we understand each other?"

She tried to speak, but her ability to do so was nearly gone.

"Just nod yes or no," I said. I was getting impatient with her and ready to express it again physically. What had gotten into me? I suppose it was that nobody, and I meant nobody, threatened my mother, or they were going to face the consequences.

Lisa quickly nodded, and I tied her hands and legs together, and then I secured her to our heavy couch.

This crazed killer wasn't going anywhere.

"Now, call the chief, and I'll call an ambulance for Frank. With any luck, they'll be able to get to him in time."

It was all oddly anticlimactic after Momma and I made our calls.

As we waited for the reinforcements to arrive, I said, "Thanks for stopping me."

"I was afraid that you couldn't even hear me," she said. "It was honestly the most frightened I'd been all night, and that's saying something."

"We don't have to go into too much detail when we talk about that part of it, do we?" In all honesty, I was a little embarrassed about how I'd behaved.

"Your secret is safe with me," she said.

"What about her?" I asked as I looked down at Lisa.

"She can say whatever she wants to. After all, who's going to believe her?"

When the chief got there, he rushed to Momma first. "Are you okay?" he asked her gently.

She was holding a dishtowel to her neck. "I just got a few scratches, but if it hadn't been for Suzanne, I would have been dead."

"That's only fitting," I said, "because I'm the one who got you in trouble in the first place." I turned to the chief as I added, "I don't know if you heard, but Lisa attacked her husband before she came over here."

"I know," the chief said as he nodded. "The EMTs got to Frank in time. It turns out that he's a tough man to kill, no thanks to her." Before he took care of Lisa, he asked me, "How about you? Are you all right, Suzanne?"

"I'm fine," I said. "I'm just a little shaky right now."

"That's to be expected," he said, and then the police chief started untying Lisa from my thorough bounds. As he slipped the cuffs on her, he said, "I don't want any trouble from you, do you understand?"

She had no more fight in her.

Evidently I'd choked it right out of her.

Officer Grant, my friend and a loyal donut customer, came rushing in with his gun drawn. When he saw that everything was under control, he quickly holstered it again.

"Take her to the station and lock her up," the chief commanded.

"Are you two all right?" he asked us as he pulled Lisa to her feet.

"We're both fine," Momma said.

Officer Grant grinned. "Maybe so, but it looks like your towel is leaking. Should I call for another ambulance, Chief?"

"Do it," Chief Martin said.

"Phillip, you know how I hate to ride in those things. Can't you take me yourself?"

"Of course I can," he said, and then he turned to me. "Are you coming?"

"I'll drive Suzanne there," Grace said as she burst in. "She can tell me what happened on the way to the hospital."

"Is that okay with you, Momma?" I asked her gently.

"It's fine, Suzanne. Thank you saving me."

I got closer and whispered, "Thank *you* for saving *me*."

Momma just patted my hand, and then she said, "Let's go, Phillip."

"Yes, ma'am," he said as he led her outside.

"So, what did I miss?" Grace asked with a grin.

"You drive, and I'll catch you up," I said. "I'm afraid that my hands would shake too much."

"I'm your gal," she said. "I'm guessing there will be no donuts tomorrow, am I right?"

I'd completely forgotten about the next day's work. "I'll call Emma on the way and ask her and her mother to step in. They've done it for me before."

As we walked outside to her car, Grace said, "Suzanne, you know that it's okay if the donut shop closes every now and then, don't you?"

"Not on my watch," I said with a grin. "Especially not now."

"Why not now?" she asked.

"Because it will be the last day that Donut Hearts is ever open," I said, knowing in my heart that it was the right decision to make.

"You're going, then?" Grace asked me.

"If tonight taught me anything, it's how precious life is. I don't want to spend another minute of it away from Jake if I don't have to." I hugged her, and then I said, "As much as I'll miss you, this is just something that I have to do. Do you think Momma will understand?"

"Suzanne, we both know that your mother just wants you to be happy, no matter where that leads you."

"Then I guess I'd better call Jake and tell him the good news."

After I called Emma and made arrangements to have her and her mother open the donut shop, I called Jake. To my delight, he picked up on the first ring. I hadn't talked to him in several hours, but now I had something to say.

"Suzanne, I was just about to call you myself. What are you, a mind reader?"

"Me first," I said. "Jake, I've given this a lot of thought. There are a ton of reasons for me to stay in April Springs and go on making donuts until I'm old and gray, but there's only one good reason that I don't want to anymore. I've been able to handle things the way they are with you traveling the state and not being able to see you all of the time, but this is too much. I want to be with you, and if that means closing my shop and moving to Alaska, then so be it. I'll tell you what happened that made me come to that conclusion in a second, but first, I need to ask you a question. Do you still want me in Alaska with you?"

"No, as a matter of fact, I don't."

I dropped the phone and didn't hear the next thing that he had to say. When I picked it back up, I could hear him say, "Suzanne, are you there?"

"You don't want me!" I cried out in anguish. "I thought we were past all that."

"If you'd give me a second to explain, I'd tell you," he said. "I don't want you in Alaska with me because I'm not there anymore."

"What are you talking about?" I asked him through my tears.

"The funding fell through at the last second, and I was

ordered back to Raleigh immediately." He paused a moment, and then Jake added, "Were you really going to give up everything to join me?"

"I wouldn't be giving *you* up," I said. "When can I see you?"

"I'll be there in five minutes."

"Go to the hospital instead," I said.

"Suzanne, did something happen? Are you hurt?"

"I'm fine, but Momma got nicked up. I'll tell you once I see you. Jake, I'm so happy."

"That makes two of us," he said, and then, just before he hung up, he added, "I love you."

"I love you, too."

After I hung up, I turned to Grace and I saw her staring at me. "Wow, that was touch and go there for a minute, wasn't it?"

"You're telling me," I said.

"I take it that your boyfriend is heading back to town," she said with a smile.

"He is," I agreed happily.

"So then, you're *not* selling the donut shop and deserting me?"

"Not in the foreseeable future," I answered with a grin.

"Good. It's not that I wasn't wishing you well, but I'm sure glad that you're staying."

"You know what? So am I. I was willing to go, but I'm so much happier to be right here where I am."

"That's just outstanding," she said, and then we were finally at the hospital.

To my surprise, Emily Hargraves was waiting out front.

As I got out of Grace's car, Emily hugged me. "Suzanne, are you okay?"

"I'm fine, Emily, maybe besides a cracked rib or two."

"Did Lisa do that to you?" Emily asked.

"No, but I think you just might have," I answered,

trying to get my breath.

She laughed as she released her grip on me. "I was so worried when I heard what happened."

"Does everyone in town already know what happened?" I asked. I knew that word got around fast in our town, but that must have been some kind of record.

"It's everywhere," Emily said. "When I thought that you might have been injured, or even dying somewhere, I couldn't believe how stupidly I behaved."

"Take it easy on yourself," I said. "It couldn't have been easy for you hearing me question you."

"It wasn't, but I overreacted. This wedding has just got me so frazzled that I'm not myself anymore. By the way, I've decided to call it off," she added softly.

"Oh, no," I said as I hugged her myself. "It wasn't because of me, was it?"

"No. Yes. Well, maybe partly. Mostly though, it was because of the way that I was behaving. I was rushing things; I can see that now. I need some time before I'm truly ready."

"Have you told Max?" I asked. I had a hunch that my ex-husband would not react well to the news of the cancellation.

"He's all for it," Emily said with a grin. "He claims that when I *am* ready, then he gets to have another bachelor party."

"That sounds just like Max," I said, and then I held Emily's hands in mine as I asked, "Are you sure that you're okay with your decision?"

"I am," she said. "If and when I do get married, I don't want to do it this way. Max can wait. He told me that he's a patient man."

"He really *must* have changed," I said, laughing. To my joy, Emily joined in.

"Okay, maybe there a *few* things that I'm still working on with him," she said.

Grace stepped forward and said, "I hate to butt in, but

your mother would like to see you."

I looked around for my boyfriend, but he was still nowhere in sight.

"Don't worry about Jake. I'll stay out here and tell him what happened," Grace said.

"Thanks. That would be great," I replied. Grace would tell him as much as she knew, but I would have to tell him the rest of it. I'd thought about keeping my flash of deadly anger from him, but he deserved to know. I just wouldn't feel right keeping something like that to myself.

As I walked into the emergency room, I couldn't help wondering how things might have turned out differently, and tonight my life would have been ruined and wrecked beyond repair. I was lucky to have my mother safe, and Jake back to boot, and I was grateful.

Being rejected by Jude had driven Lisa over the edge, and to my surprise, a little bit of me sympathized with her. I'd felt the sting of being turned away when I'd thought that Jake was going to dump me, and it hadn't been nice.

But that's where our paths differed.

Lisa had struck out at everyone involved in anger, and I had tried my best to accept the truth and move on with my life.

And in the end, that was what finally separated the two of us.

She'd chosen death, and I'd opted for life.

In the end, I liked to think that we each got what we deserved.

RECIPES

Chocolate Cranberry Cinnamon Donuts

Lately, I've been experimenting with donuts made on the quick, and I've come up with a few truly good and easy variations of old themes. When I have a craving for something different, I wander through the baking aisles at the grocery store looking for new ingredients to use. I've found that companies such as Martha White have premade muffin and biscuit mixes that can be modified to make wonderful donuts quickly. For example, this new family favorite uses a basic cinnamon biscuit mix, and with a few additions, these donuts become something spectacular. To a basic 7-ounce mix, I add dried cranberries, semisweet chocolate chips, and household sugar to sweeten the treats. The drop donuts created are wonderful fried, and for an extra treat, we like to top these with a chocolate drizzle followed by a sprinkling of powdered sugar, making them decadent and delicious. This goes under the Very Easy file!

INGREDIENTS

1 packet (7 ounces) biscuit mix (we like cinnamon, but chocolate chip work, too)
1/2 cup whole milk
1/4 cup dried cranberries (raisins will work as well)
2 tablespoons semisweet chocolate chips
2 tablespoons granulated sugar

INSTRUCTIONS

In a medium-sized bowl, add the mix, sugar, and milk, stirring until the dry ingredients are incorporated into the wet, but being careful not to overstir. Next, add the dried cranberries and chocolate chips, mixing them in as well.

Drop bits of dough using a small-sized cookie scoop (the size of your thumb, approximately). Fry in hot canola oil (360 to 370 degrees F) for 3 to 4 minutes, turning halfway through.

Yields 10–12 donut drops.

Enhanced Fruit and Pancake Surprises

I've also tried other mixes besides the ones for biscuits and muffins. For example, pancake mixes can make a very good donut when augmented with some of your favorite fruits. I've done these with peaches and mangos, but my family likes mashed bananas and cubed apples in the batter, creating a type of fritter on the fly. These are surprisingly good, and easy to make, so give them a try.

INGREDIENTS

1 cup pancake mix
1/2 cup buttermilk
1 egg, beaten
1/4 cup granulated sugar
1 teaspoon vanilla extract
Canola oil for frying (the amount depends on your pot or fryer)

INSTRUCTIONS

In a bowl, mix the pancake mix, buttermilk, egg, sugar, and vanilla extract to a decently smooth consistency.

Drop bits of the batter using a small-sized cookie scoop (the size of your thumb, approximately) or two spoons into the hot oil. Fry at 360 to 370 degrees F for 3 to 4 minutes, flipping halfway through.

Yields 6–8 donut drops.

Variations on the Enhanced Fruit and Pancake Surprises Recipe

If you're feeling especially adventurous, as we sometimes are, I reserve some of the basic pancake batter before I add any fruit from the previous recipe and use it as a coating for sliced bananas and apples. This gets a little messy when you dip them, but they are delicious. Simply dip the banana slice or apple into the batter, then fry for a minute or two until the treat is golden in hue. We like these dipped in chocolate or sprinkled with cinnamon sugar before eating, but they also make a nice little side item for the donuts listed above.

INGREDIENTS

1/4 to 1/2 cup of the enhanced batter in the previous recipe before fruit is added
1 medium apple, peeled, cored, and sliced
1 ripe banana, sliced into half-inch sections
Canola oil for frying (the amount depends on your pot or fryer)

Toppings
Chocolate sauce, heated
Cinnamon sugar, made up of 2 tablespoons granulated sugar mixed with 2 teaspoons cinnamon

INSTRUCTIONS

Prepare the fruit, dip it in the enhanced batter, and then fry for 2 minutes, flipping halfway through.

Yields as many slices as you like.

AFTERWORD

Dear Reader,

I hope that you've enjoyed my latest donut mystery. Thanks again for joining me on another new adventure with Suzanne, Grace, Momma, and the rest of the gang in April Springs, North Carolina. Some of you have noticed that I've cut back on the recipes offered in each book. That's in direct response to a great deal of mail I've gotten recently that the number of recipes has been a bit overwhelming, in some cases even detracting from the mystery itself. That was never my intent, so in response, I've decreased the number of recipes in each book. Also, there have been several comments that the recipes mixed within the chapters is distracting and interrupts the flow of the story itself, so I'm moving them all to one place in the back of the book.

In addition, I've had quite a few folks say that they would like my donut books to be a bit shorter, more along the lines of my diner and ghost cat mysteries. Keeping that in mind, I've cut a few scenes in order to provide you all with a more compact novel that I trust you will enjoy.

I hope that you approve of these changes, especially since they have the added cumulative benefit of allowing me to provide *more* books in the future for your reading pleasure. In particular, the recipes take a great deal of time, and I discard many recipes for every one that I end up using. That will leave me more time for creating fiction and exploring the worlds we've been enjoying together.

And finally, I'd like to take this time to thank you all for reading these mysteries that I have so much fun creating. They are a delight for me to write, but without you on the other end, they would be nothing more than me shouting into a hurricane, barely heard and quickly forgotten.

Until we meet again, I wish you all the best,

The Author

If you enjoy Jessica Beck Mysteries and would like to be notified when the next book is being released, please send your e-mail address to **newreleases@jessicabeckmysteries.net**. Your e-mail address will not be shared, sold, bartered, traded, broadcast, or disclosed in any way. There will be no spam from us, just a friendly reminder when the latest book is being released.

Made in United States
North Haven, CT
23 November 2022

27164038R00119